A Less Convenient Arrangement

CONVENIENT RISK SERIES, BOOK 7

SARA R. TURNQUIST

MOUNTAIN
SUMMIT PRESS

If you would like to stay up-to-date on this and other series from Sara and receive a free ebook, sign up for her newsletter:

https://saraturnquist.com/list

*For anyone who has faced trials
and come out the other side.*

CHAPTER 1
Scorned

The world had lost its sheen. Its vibrancy. Its life.

Sadie Rose Perkins stared at the ceiling and was dreading yet another day. How could she face the people of Wharton City with their accusations and stares? How could she face her life?

Couldn't she just turn over and let sleep claim her once more? Perhaps permanently? Nothing about this was fair. Perhaps. Did she have this coming?

How had she not seen it? She should have.

Had it only been a week since she woke to find her father gone? As if that hadn't been heartbreaking enough, the following days brought with them an even greater distress—the revelation that the man she had trusted, the town's once prominent and respected banker, had embezzled from the bank. Really, from the good people of this town.

He had betrayed everyone. Everyone. Even her. Yes, she should have noticed that something was off. Somehow.

Would the townsfolk ever forgive her? How could they?

Perhaps she deserved as much. She should have seen the signs.

Father had been more distant, absorbed with matters of the bank. And he had been home less and less. Even then, he often closed himself in his study.

How had she not seen? Not suspected?

Yes, she had earned blame in this.

If only she could apologize enough. But no one would hear it. Scowls and narrowed gazes were the common greeting now. And would continue to be.

Sadie covered her face. What was the point?

Outside her open bedroom door, movement in the great room drew her attention. Mother.

The woman had been agitated. Even more so than usual. This whole situation had indeed taken its toll on the older woman. If only Sadie could shield her mother. From the burden. From the shame.

Sliding her feet from what little warmth the covers offered, Sadie shivered. Still, she forced herself to sit and press her vulnerable soles to the cold wood. A chill shot through her—right up her spine. But she had to push on. Mother needed her.

She grabbed her knit shawl, a precious gift that reminded Sadie of a time when her mother was more capable, and pulled it around her shoulders. While it did nothing for her cold feet, perhaps it would keep her upper body from freezing. Padding into the great room, she found her mother by a shelf. As she watched, the woman lifted a book, flipped through the pages, and tossed the volume to the floor, only to pick up another from its perch.

"Mother? What's the matter?" Sadie crossed the room and set a hand to her mother's arm.

The woman turned a hollow gaze on Sadie. "I...can't seem to find your father."

Sadie's heart dropped. Not this again.

Shifting her focus back to her task, her mother said, "I know he left a map. I just can't find it." Her hands shook as she poured over the next book.

Reaching for the hands that had done much to comfort her over the years, Sadie attempted to still the tremors. Mother's fingers were as ice. How long had she been up and about? Sadie lifted the book from her mother's reach.

It seemed at first that Mother would protest. She opened her mouth, and her lips moved as if she spoke, but no sound came forth.

"You must be cold." Sadie tugged at the older woman.

Mother stood her ground, but her gaze set on Sadie once more. If only the stare wasn't so vacant.

Sadie's heart squeezed.

Then there was a spark in Mother's eyes. "Shouldn't you be getting ready for school?"

Sadie frowned. She never quite knew what to do in these moments. They had become more frequent of late. Since Father's flight in the night, Mother had been in a constant state of confusion it seemed.

"Mother, I finished school. Two years ago."

The woman's graying hair was tangled. Sadie would have to do something about that. And her thin, frayed nightgown needed attention.

Deep brown eyes looked about Sadie's features. Did she try to discern the truth? Could she? "School is over? Then I should get supper on the table."

Mother pulled free. Then she walked across the cluttered area, stumbling over the pile of books, and moved toward her bedroom.

Sadie paused, taking in a deep breath and releasing it. Then she followed.

Her mother stood in front of an open wardrobe. "Now where are the potatoes?"

"In the kitchen." Sadie could not help the moisture building behind her eyes. "Mother, let me help you get something warmer on…"

"I can't seem to find the potatoes." She whirled toward Sadie, that empty look about her again.

Time to try a different tactic. One that usually worked. But Sadie regretted resorting to it. She just couldn't do this. Not right now. Hadn't she earned a moment of peace? Just for a minute? "Mother, we had supper."

"Oh?" The woman's confusion intensified. As did Sadie's distress.

"Yes," Sadie forced her voice to stay calm. "It's time to lay down."

Mother's gaze slid to the window. "It's so bright."

"Yes, it is. But it will be dark soon." She laid gentle hands on Mother's shoulders and prodded her in the direction of the bed. "You have a big day tomorrow, and you need your sleep."

"What about your father?" Even as she protested, Mother sat on the edge of the mattress. "I need to—"

"I'll take care of Father. You rest."

Though there wasn't so much as a hint of certainty in Mother's eyes, the woman lay down and let Sadie pull the covers to her chin.

"Just for a minute."

"All right, Ma, just for a minute."

Then the woman closed her eyes.

Sadie tiptoed across the floor as quietly as possible so that she was in the hall before she fell apart. She shoved her fist against her mouth to muffle her sobs as she sank to the floor.

David Anderson looked around the ranch from his position on the homestead's porch. How did one survive here? It was so...dirty. Not that the dirt would kill him, but he definitely preferred paved roads and fine rooms. This was nothing like Richmond. He longed for the day he would wave goodbye to this place, see it in the distance, and welcome normalcy.

This next week couldn't pass fast enough. How Aunt Sylvia continued to convince him to delay their return was beyond him. No more. They would be on that train come Wednesday. No matter what.

Brandon Miller meandered out of the barn with one of his ranch hands...what was his name again? There was little need to keep up with them all. It wasn't as if he'd be seeing them again after next Wednesday. No harm in just nodding in their direction, was there?

But as Brandon approached the house, stepping up to the porch, he eyed his cousin. How were they, two rather different people, related? Brandon loved all these rustic things. He had been born to privilege and rejected it for this harsh land and hard ways. Calloused hands and rope burn indeed. It was beyond him why anyone would make such a choice.

And he couldn't be more grateful for what he had back in Richmond. This, most certainly, was not the life for him. Others might consider his life too soft. Let them. He enjoyed his comfort and the society of the big city.

"How's your day been?" Brandon murmured. Did he truly feel the need to exchange pleasantries?

David looked up to see Brandon standing near the front door. By himself. Where had that ranch hand gone? It seemed David and his cousin were alone. How he hated these moments! They never had anything to say to one another. At least, nothing that mattered.

"It's been well enough, I suppose." It hadn't. But David had to remember his manners. He wasn't anything if not for the politeness and good nature of his breeding.

"I'm going to town later. Why don't you join me?" Brandon watched him.

Town? Why ever would he do that to himself? That small collection of buildings was no more civil than the ranch. Except...there was more to see. And perhaps he could send a telegram to his parents—assure his father that his return was imminent and let his mother know he was well.

"That sounds like a fine prospect."

Brandon looked down at the boards that made up the porch.

Did he scoff at David? Why? He could have nothing to judge David for.

But when Brandon glanced back up, he offered a half smile. "It'll be a good diversion I think."

David gazed across the bare landscape—well, bare of anything mean-ingful—and closed his eyes.

"You coming in?" Brandon's voice interrupted David's efforts to imagine he was somewhere—anywhere—else.

David looked at his cousin once again.

Brandon held the door to the homestead open and nodded in the direction of the interior. Whatever for?

Then David remembered...mealtime. So it was.

David stood and gave a jerk of his head in assent. "Lead the way."

When Brandon turned, David grimaced. How much more of these meals could he take? Cook, as they called her, was a fine help in the kitchen. At least Brandon and the ranch hands had three squares a day. But David longed for the finer cuisine he so appreciated. That was perhaps what he missed the most. Well, that and days without being covered head-to-toe in dust. Even if David stayed in the homestead, the stuff found its way everywhere onto his person.

As they stepped inside, David moved into the great room. He hoped he might grab a few moments to wash up. But he was interrupted by a distinctly feminine voice.

"I wondered where you got off to."

David turned.

Brandon's wife moved across the space, fairly gliding. Now there was something he wouldn't tire of—a fine woman with notable grace and poise. He understood that she had been raised back east. And it showed.

"I was just out on the porch. Taking in the...sights." He had learned better than to share his true feelings about this dust bowl.

"Oh?" Amanda's gaze moved between the two men. "I wished I'd have gone out to sit with you for a few moments. Oliver would have liked that."

Oh yes, the young child did enjoy playing in all that dirt. Good heavens.

Brandon moved closer to his wife and put an arm around her, drawing her to himself and pressing a kiss to the side of her face.

She batted her eyelashes and it looked as if her face flushed.

It was all David could do not to roll his eyes. Weren't they just the picture of perfection? David doubted that such truly existed. No matter how much they appeared so. He had nursed his broken heart long enough to know that hoping for something that didn't exist was useless. And wasteful. Much better to focus on things he could attain—like the partnership in his father's firm.

That mattered. That was solid. That was sure.

He smiled tightly at the couple, trying not to let his emotions show on his face. He found it difficult, so he ducked into the hall and moved into his provided sleeping space.

A quick wash made him feel more human. And a bit more himself. He glanced at his hands as he dried them—he'd found he had to wash several times a day to keep the dirt at bay. Then he touched his hair. Everything seemed in place. The pomade had gotten low. What was the point anyway? It wasn't as if he would be seen by anyone of any consequence. So, water slicked back it was.

Sighing, he ran a hand down his shirt front. He couldn't hide in here forever; he had to go out and face this world sometime. Straightening the shirt once more, he sucked in a breath, pushed out the door, and made his way to the dining room.

He was greeted by the stench of the cows and horses. The ranch hands had joined the family in the dining space. Could he just once be spared? Maybe he would convince Brandon to stay in town and eat at the café—the only piece of civility this place seemed to offer.

Still...it didn't help him in this moment. He garnered his courage and slipped into his seat.

The filthy men, well, more overgrown boys, took their places across the table and commented on how good everything smelled.

How could they smell anything but the odors they dragged in on their boots? David certainly couldn't.

Cook and Amanda bustled about, bringing food to the table. And Cook muttered something about waiting for grace to be said before partaking.

It was an unnecessary worry. They all knew better. Even David by now.

Though that felt as useless as everything else about this place—God indeed.

Still, he smiled and bided his time until the 'vittles' would be passed.

Samuel sat beside him and offered him a smile.

That boy was a bright spot. He was interesting. And interested in the things David had to share about the world he came from. But, like Brandon, the adolescent's potential would likely be wasted on this backwoods town.

If You are listening, God. He tried. More to himself than an actual prayer. *Keep this one from such a life.*

He wished that there would be opportunity forthcoming for the boy. And when it came that he wouldn't push it aside or let it pass him by.

David could hope.

Brandon said a few words to the ranch hands and then cleared his throat. David knew what was coming.

"Let's bow our heads," Brandon said, as he reached for his wife's hand. Then he returned a simple prayer that was all well and good enough. For their purposes.

"Dig in!" Cook announced as Brandon closed his prayer.

All holds barred, the ranch hands went after the bowls and plates as if they had never seen food. It was always like that. Oh, how he wished that he wouldn't have to touch the spoons after them.

CHAPTER 2
Abandoned

T he day had not been good to her. Nor had the night that followed. Mother had more difficulty sleeping of late and was often up in the late hours.

Still, Sadie hoped she might be able to disguise just how worn she was. Looking in her mirror, she believed that was for naught. Her eyes showed it the most, the skin around creating creases that should not be there. Her dresses fit a little looser, too. Not that it surprised her. Between caring for Mother and the emotional toll of the scandal, she almost expected as much. Though, there was reason to hope.

Josiah returned today.

What would his reaction be to the happenings of the last week? She prayed he would be the steady, stable comfort for her he had always been. Besides, he loved her. He would stand by her. And without her father, both she and her mother would need Josiah to legitimize them. Else all that was Mother's would be in jeopardy. Yes, they must preserve what they did have.

And Josiah was the answer.

How different she felt about this man. She had not been thrilled when Father had granted Josiah his daughter's hand. But there was more to a marriage than feelings, than love, right? A position in the community and a family would fill her life with more than she needed. Enough, certainly, to keep her distracted.

Pinching color into lifeless cheeks, she assured herself that every hair was in place.

A knock on the door drew her attention. Had he come so soon? He wasn't due for another half hour at least.

"Yes?" Sadie called with some hesitation.

The door creaked open, and Mrs. Wallem peered in. "Miss Sadie," the woman said as she settled kind eyes on her. "Mr. Holgrew is here to see you."

Sadie let out a breath and let her hands fall into her lap. "Thank you. I will be down in a moment."

Mrs. Wallem nodded and closed the door.

Sadie met her own gaze in the looking glass. How was she going to do this? She had to put on a strong front for Josiah. In all likelihood, he had caught wind of the situation. And she must show him she could weather this storm and come out on the other side.

She pressed a smile to her features. It would have to do. There was no need to keep Josiah waiting.

Rising, she then maneuvered through the house and to the lower level. The door to the parlor was ajar, and she drew in another long breath. She could do this.

Pushing at the door, she stepped within.

Josiah's tall frame was silhouetted by the sun streaming in. His gaze appeared to be set on something beyond the room. The parlor boasted a fine prospect indeed, looking over the mountains in the distance. But he stood rather stiffly. Between the angle of the light and the turn of his countenance, she couldn't make out his features.

She let her eyes wander over his form. This was the man she had agreed to wed. And now the man who would be her and Mother's salvation. While she had not always been certain about the arrangement, she was now thankful. So very thankful.

Sadie cleared her throat.

Josiah turned, thrusting his features into sharp focus. His eyes widened at first but soon narrowed as if he studied her. What was he looking at? Or did he search *for* something? He turned to the side then faced her.

"I am...glad that you have returned. Much has happened since you—"

"I heard." The words were pressed forth. Not gentle, not comforting...just there.

She swallowed hard against a throat raw with emotion. Her eyes latched to his. No matter how much it hurt to maintain such contact, she would not turn away.

"Sadie, you..." He stepped toward her, hand lifting. Then his eyebrows furrowed. "Have you slept?"

Moisture built behind her eyes, but she blinked it away. "Yes," she said, as she looked down at the floor. She couldn't risk him seeing what the offer of tenderness did to her. "Though I confess it has been difficult."

He nodded and continued advancing until he stood an arm's length away. "I can imagine."

She sought his gaze again.

His eyes were pained. She wished she might wrap herself in his concern and find respite there. Perhaps there was more stirring in her heart for him than she'd believed.

In a moment of boldness, she closed the gap and leaned into him. The warmth of his chest gave her pause to close her eyes and rest in the moment. His hands clasped her arms. Yes, this was what she needed.

But then...why did he not hold her? Would he not welcome her as she so needed him to?

In the next moment, he eased her away from himself.

Thankful for his sense of propriety, she still could not deny her regret to lose the comfort of his physical support.

"Sadie, I..." His words faded, and he cleared his throat.

She looked up at him, but he dodged her gaze.

"What is it?" Her words were soft. And her heart stuttered. What did he intend to say?

He licked his lips.

"If you are worried about the engagement party, I...don't need one. After all, I care not for grandeur and pomp. Just having you here is—"

"It's not the party." His words lacked force. Indeed, they were more of a harsh whisper.

Telling herself she needed to assure him of her regard—however strong or weak it was—she set a hand to his forearm.

He looked down at her fingers and used his opposite hand to cover hers. Again, his touch offered something she needed, but it wasn't enough. Then he lifted her hand from his arm and stared down at her. "Sadie, I need you to understand..."

As his voice trailed, dread crept into the edges of her mind. What did she need to understand?

"I care for you a great deal."

This she knew. She had seen it in his eyes many times and felt it in his touch. Though, not today. This was different. This was something else. But what?

"And I..." she paused before finishing, "I care for you."

After all, isn't that how a betrothed couple need feel for each other? Did it matter that she didn't feel for him as he wished? Nor to the depth he felt for her? She could grow to love him. She was determined she could.

"But..." he sucked in a breath and glanced in the direction of the window again.

What was he not saying? Could she bear for him to drag this out?

"But what?" Fear found its way into her voice. Even she heard the break in her tone.

"I...can't do this." He pushed her hand away.

She pulled her arm back to herself as if burned. "Can't what?"

"You can't expect me to...for us to...for things to be the way they were."

She widened her eyes, unable to tear her gaze from his. How could this be? He cared for her. She knew he did. Surely her newfound situation couldn't change that.

"Let's be realistic, Sadie." He glared at her. Gone was the tenderness and compassion she had believed she saw. Now there was hardness and resolve. "You can't hold me to this...arrangement."

Hold *him* to the arrangement? Did he wish to be set free from their betrothal? An *arrangement* he had insisted on just one month ago?

She let her gaze wander over his features, seeing only pain and—was it true?—scorn. Suddenly, it didn't matter that she would be left with precious few, if any, options. She would never...

"You can't." He pushed out. "And I won't be bound to...it," he finished weakly.

Her. He had meant to say *bound to her*.

She turned as hot tears blurred her vision.

"Sadie, I..." His voice took on a pleading tone. "I'm sorry it has to be this way."

She didn't respond. In truth, what could she say? Was there anything she might speak that would change his mind? She bit at her lip...she would not cry in front of him.

"I'm...sorry." Shuffling behind her and to the side told that he moved toward the parlor's entrance. She followed his footfalls until the grand front door slammed behind him.

Finally. Out of that house. That small, rustic abode. Little more than a glorified cabin. David Anderson couldn't quite name what it was about the property that felt so confining. Yes, the homestead wasn't sprawling, but the land was. Not that a walk about that dusty place fell on his list of things to do. Not with these shoes. How was one supposed to live like this? Even the town seemed limiting. But it did give some semblance of society. Though not much.

David strolled down the boardwalk in front of the General Store. And groaned. Dust was everywhere. Everywhere.

Still, he had room to breathe. To think. And to struggle with his impatience.

Why would his aunt wish to linger? He had reached his tolerance for this backwards place, how had she not? It was time to return home. His father needed him. The firm needed him. And he needed the civility and refinement of Richmond. Yes, he would have to speak with Aunt Sylvia again. Firmly. Remind her of their plans and insist they keep them this time.

He neared the telegraph office. His one real task today, and the reason he begged off staying at the livery with Brandon—to pick up the mail and check for packages. But as he entered the building that was smaller yet than any other, he faced a line of townsfolk. And the office shrunk a bit more. Wonderful.

What could he do but step to the end of the small gathering?

It would not do for him to grumble. That would be unseemly. So, he glanced over the posted notices and read everything in sight. Still the line did not move. Tuning in to the woman at the front, it became apparent she relayed an entirely unnecessary narrative to the agent.

David fought the ire rising in his throat. Why him?

A presence behind had him turning. The young woman who came in and settled in line after him had red rimmed eyes and a rather disheveled appearance. But as he took her in, he noted her delicate features and large brown eyes. Quite attractive. Not that he intended to become entangled in anything beyond simple appreciation. He nodded and refocused his attention on the busybody at the front.

However, the others in line ahead kept looking back and staring at the woman. Or at least, he assumed that was so. Surely, they didn't find *him* a curiosity. Their gazes were hard and the turn of their countenances dismissive. Was the woman a social pariah of some sort?

He inched forward. Best to create as much separation as possible.

But something tugged in his chest. She seemed so forlorn. And lost. While her clothing and manner spoke to a refinement beyond what he experienced thus far in the small town. What cause could these people have to shun her? What could she have done to merit such?

Something whispered that these answers could be varied in content and number. And none of them would grant him the space or reason to cross that barrier erected by the steely glares.

Still, as he waited, his conscience hounded him. It wasn't as if he truly cared what these townsfolk thought. He'd be out of here in six days. Never to return.

The people ahead whispered; casting looks in her direction again.

As if they were so perfect.

He sensed movement behind, and he shifted to look at her once more.

The lady stepped out of line, covering the lower portion of her face with a handkerchief. Would she let these gossiping hens dissuade her from her errand?

With a boldness that surprised even him, he reached for her arm.

She jerked back at the contact. Her eyes widened as they settled on him. Indeed, they were puffy. The tears that fell here and now were not the first of the day.

Audible gasps sounded from further toward the front.

"Pardon, Miss..." he prompted, hoping for her name.

She just stared. Her lips parted, then sealed.

"If your time is short, please allow me to offer you my place in line."

Again, her mouth moved, but nothing came forth.

The murmurs and whispers surged.

He whirled toward the sound. "If I were you, I'd make quite certain I was sinless before casting stones."

The women stopped their clucking and stared, now at him. Great. Heat from the intensity on that one side caused warmth to crawl into his face. He was tempted to move closer to the nameless woman who continued to watch him.

He urged her forward and in front of him. "Please, miss. I insist."

She complied without a word. Was she mute? Certainly a 'thank you' or some sign of gratitude was in order.

Instead, she shifted and faced away from him. That left her looking at the small crowd of gossipers whose eyes bore into her.

He raised a brow and tilted his head, sending a warning shot to the cluster.

They turned back toward the service window, and all was silent.

At last, some peace.

Only...as he stared at the haphazardly coiffed cinnamon hair of the woman before him, he noted that her shoulders quivered. Was she not done crying? Would she not take better care? The thought of what it would be like to touch the shiny locks slipped through his awareness. Stuff and nonsense! There was not allowance for such. He refused to permit that mental trail to carry him any further.

This was a filthy town with nothing but tiresome people. The sooner he could leave, the better. And nothing...not even the silken appearance of fine hair would dissuade him.

CHAPTER 3
The Banker's Daughter

David sighed. The trip into town was for naught. Nothing about it was redeeming. In fact, the chance encounter with the woman had hindered him. Even now, she crept into his thoughts.

All he had to do, however, was remember the look in Claire's eyes when she informed him of her betrayal. That should be enough to give him more than a pause when it came to women, crippled as his trust had become.

The wagon—a terrible and most uncomfortable contraption that it was—rolled along the padded-out path to the homestead. He and Brandon had not said two words to each other since departing. Should he introduce a topic? Or just let the awkward silence continue? They hadn't really had any conversation worthwhile since his arrival two months ago.

"Were you able to send your telegram?" Brandon's question shocked him. So, the man did sense the strangeness of their silence.

"I...did. But it took some time." That had certainly been true. He had never planned to stand in that small space for so long. But what else could he do? It seemed nothing could light a fire under that agent.

"Ah. It gets awful busy at times." Brandon's attention remained fixed on the horse in front of them.

"Yes. I noticed." After speaking, David realized that his statement might well end the conversation. Then they would be back to the terrible stalemate. So uncomfortable. He continued, "There was one woman who seemed rather...on the outside."

"Oh?" Brandon leaned back against the bench. He appeared only mildly amused.

"She seemed some sort of object of scorn. I can't imagine what put her in such a predicament. Not that the people of Wharton City have other things to distract themselves from such dramatics."

Brandon looked at him. He did not appear pleased.

"I mean," David started, wanting to placate his cousin. He had not intended to be so insulting. Though what he said had been true. "There doesn't seem to be many goings on of any import. People must find something to fill their time."

That did not help. And though Brandon turned back to the horse, David sensed he did not appreciate David's words.

"Folks have a lot of work in this place. They don't have time for the things that concern people in the larger cities. Certainly no time to make much ado about socializing." Brandon's response was curt. "In fact, I find that I enjoy the absence of such theatrics."

Theatrics? Were the inter-workings of social engagement and inter-action such a bore to him? How could Brandon have gone from high society with its pomp and excitement to this stale town, bereft of anything truly interesting?

Although, the telegraph office had not been completely devoid of theatrics. "That woman certainly drew a lot of attention and specula-tion from the more...mundane townsfolk."

One of Brandon's eyebrows rose. "Oh?"

David took that as curiosity. "Yes. A young woman. With light brown hair. She seemed rather out of place."

"You must be talking about Sadie Perkins." Brandon's response was brief, simple, decided.

Though how much ado could there be in such a small place? There could only be one woman in the whole town as interesting and talked about. "Perhaps. What...um..." David cleared his throat and attempted to filter his words. Not that there was much cause. He didn't truly care. Only curious himself. "What is her story?"

Brandon didn't so much as flinch. If he did discern anything beyond a simple inquiry, he didn't let on.

"She's the banker's daughter." His responses were getting shorter.

"And that merits such behavior from the townspeople? Do they not care for anyone who has the gall to rise above?"

Brandon shot him a look. His thoughts were difficult to discern. He seemed simultaneously amused and confused.

"I don't see why everyone should look down on her because her father has money." But something in David whispered there must be more to it. She had been crying...even before she entered the telegraph office filled with onlookers.

"Her father skipped town with everyone's money."

It all closed in. The banker had been a no-account. And his flawed character would be visited upon the daughter...for some reason. Not that the society of Richmond would have behaved any differently. It was the way of things. Though...something about it didn't seem fair. The woman's features had testified of her weariness and wariness. How much should one have to pay for the sins of another?

Brandon spoke up again. "But it doesn't make it right...what everyone is saying. How they treat her."

David considered Brandon's words that only affirmed David's own thoughts. It wasn't right. The young woman did not need to pay for her father's unscrupulous conduct. She needed someone to step in—as he had today—and show the townsfolk that she wasn't to blame. Someone like him.

Now that was ludicrous. He was catching a train out of here in a matter of days. There was little he might do to change the town's opinion in that time. Yes, he had done what he could by defending her earlier today. Maybe his words would stick with those women who had judged her unfairly. And his own good reputation would deflect some of their bad opinion.

He had done all he could do.

CHAPTER 4
Hopeless

S adie stepped through the front door of the grand house she called home. Perhaps, it would not be so for much longer. But she couldn't think about that right now. There were other things to focus on. Things that pertained to the wellbeing of her mother and herself.

She sighed. Would this nightmare ever end? One day, she was moving with the current that drove the world around her. The next, she was fighting to keep her head above the waves. Everything fell on her shoulders the minute her father took all that money. And the responsibility weighed like an anchor.

Just then she noticed that Mrs. Wallem had not greeted her. And that the house was quiet. Perhaps too quiet. Where was the kindly woman? Where was Mother? Had something happened?

She opened her mouth to call out but thought better of it. Instead, she slipped through the house and toward her mother's bedroom.

Peering into the darkened room, she spotted her mother lying on the bed, covers drawn. What had happened?

Someone tapped on her shoulder.

She whirled, gasping as she fell against the wall.

"Miss Sadie, I am so sorry. I didn't mean to frighten you." Mrs. Wallem's eyes were wide.

Sadie set a hand to her chest. If only she could command the intense pounding to cease. "It is all right. I was...just checking on Mother."

Mrs. Wallem frowned, and the lines in her face seemed to deepen. She looked as tired as Sadie felt. They had both been through much these last days, tending for Mother and grabbing sleep when they could.

"How is she?" Sadie dared to ask.

Mrs. Wallem's gaze shifted in the direction of Mother's bed. "She was rather agitated this afternoon."

Sadie nodded. Such was the way of it these days. She didn't like that Mother was asleep already, for it would make for a long night. Though she couldn't fault Mrs. Wallem. No doubt the woman had reached the end of her ability to manage Mother. The laudanum was always the last resort. And needed more and more each day that passed.

"How did you fare?" There was hope in Mrs. Wallem's eyes. Might there be respite in sight?

"I sent the telegram to Aunt Jane. There is nothing now but to await her response." Sadie wished she had better news. She would have to check the telegraph office often to see if either her aunt or cousin could come and assist. And did they ever need the help! Still, frequent trips into town did not appeal. She prayed the answer would be forthcoming and soon.

Sadie nodded to Mrs. Wallem. "Please, rest. You've earned it."

"Not right now. The dinner hour approaches. I should get something started."

"I can manage," Sadie offered. Sure, she could. The only instruction in the kitchen she had ever received was of a supervisory nature. Her father never intended that she would be cooking. Ever.

Mrs. Wallem shot her a look that told she knew as much.

Sadie shook her head. "If I can't, I'll find something when I get hungry."

The woman lingered in indecision for a moment. And Sadie wanted to order Mrs. Wallem to bed. What would it take?

"Trust me," Sadie said, setting a hand on Mrs. Wallem's shoulder. "I can do that much."

That seemed to satisfy the woman for she nodded and turned, moving down the hallway.

After the only help Sadie had in the world vanished around the corner, she deflated into a nearby chair. Too much of too much. There was always more to do. It didn't help either that everywhere she turned something was amiss.

A familiar moisture pressed into her eyes. Would she be given to tears yet again?

Straightening her posture, she wiped at her face, making every attempt to gather her emotions. Falling apart yet again would not do. She had to be stronger than this. For she had an inkling this was only the beginning.

That thought almost undid her.

But she pressed down her sadness once more and stood. She should find her own bed and make the most of the time she had to rest. Who knew what the night would bring?

As she crossed through the great room, her thoughts drifted back to the telegraph office and the man who had spoken up on her behalf. Had she seen him before? She wasn't certain. But didn't she know everyone in the area? Though, she understood many had visitors and family in town. Perhaps he was kin to someone.

Not that it mattered. While she appreciated the kindness, she would not lean into hope in that regard. Her heart was too broken and too raw to allow for anything else. It would be best if she didn't get used to the idea of someone standing by her side against the gossip mongers.

And what had she done? Stared back. Not even a simple thank you. That was unforgivable. She leaned against her door frame as she envisioned the interaction in her mind. She'd been rude...at the very least.

Still, he did make quite the picture—his warm eyes lit in passionate flair and his perfect posture disrupted. All for her sake—someone he didn't know the first thing about. The protective surge in him had soothed the ache within her. She'd gotten used to being looked over, around, and through. If anyone saw her, it was to scorn or reject her.

A pang shot through her chest. Josiah's dismissal had hurt. Not as deeply as if she had cared for him beyond the hope of rescue. But enough. Him turning a blind eye also meant there would be more trouble in the days to come. What was Mother's to retain? What might be taken away? Would Mother's ailing mind be found out and all lost?

These things would be better—almost palatable—if there were a safe place for her mother. But if anyone discovered just how much Mother had lost her sense, Sadie wouldn't be able to stop her commitment to an asylum.

That thought scared Sadie more than anything else in this situation. She had heard little about such places, but what she had discovered terrified her. Even then, the fear curled through her, winding around her heart. No matter what it took, she would fight for Mother. Sadie was determined she would keep Mother safe.

Now slipping into her room, Sadie looked at the bed. She would be more comfortable if she removed her clothes and put on a night shift. But she lacked the energy. Indeed, she cared very little for the comfort of her sleeping clothes. And only for what the bed could offer.

Throwing herself onto the mattress, she didn't even bother with the covers.

Now, if she could quiet her thoughts. But her mind rushed through the day, everything playing out before her mind's eye—all of it. And while she fought to push it to the side, she only found fitful sleep when her body's fatigue overcame her racing thoughts. And she welcomed the darkness.

David pushed food around on his plate. Was it even edible? Though he had seen the ranch hands consume it fast enough, he wasn't certain. Again, he reminded himself that Cook was good enough at putting together a meal. Perhaps he simply tired of the same flavors and foods.

"What do you think she will do?" Amanda's voice broke through his thoughts.

Brandon shook his head.

Who were they speaking of? And why did it seem as if Amanda was disturbed?

"Mrs. Perkins sure is in a way, though," Cook said as she set a hand on her husband's.

"In a way?" Amanda shot her a look. "What do you mean?"

Cook glanced at those seated around the table. The ranch hands were in their own conversation. And David peered down at his food, pretending he had no interest in their words. In truth, it surprised that he did find reason to follow their conversation.

Cook lowered her voice. "Mrs. Wallem told me that something isn't right with Mrs. Perkins' mind."

Amanda glanced at Brandon. "Poor Sadie."

Sadie? Wasn't that the name Brandon mentioned when David had asked after the young woman he'd assisted? The one with the silken brown strands and fine dress? He leaned forward into the interchange but kept his head down.

Brandon put his arm around his wife. Why was Amanda so disturbed?

"I understand your heart for her," Cook said. "And perhaps we can make some extra for dinner and take it to them. But, as far as the other, there is little we can do to help."

Amanda nodded. The emotion in her eyes was evident. "It's just...I think about how I felt when...when I didn't know what would happen to us—Samuel and me." Her lip quivered.

What did she mean? David had come to understand that Samuel wasn't truly Brandon's son, that Amanda lost her first husband to consumption. Was that the hopeless situation she referred to? How long had she been on her own before she and Brandon married?

David wanted to ask but didn't wish to let on that he had been listening.

"Though, she has Josiah Holgrew." Brandon spoke up. "When they marry, things will right themselves." He rubbed Amanda's shoulder as if that would fix anything.

Amanda gazed at her husband. It didn't take a mind reader to see the gratitude on her features.

"Oh, that's not going to happen either." Cook leaned in. "He broke the engagement."

"He didn't." Amanda slanted her body toward Cook's.

Cook nodded. "I guess he didn't want to get caught up in that scandal."

Brandon grimaced and shook his head.

"I wish there were something we could do to help," Amanda looked at her hands on the table's surface. "Anything."

David felt eyes on him. He glanced over to find Brandon watching him. Had David given away his interest in their interchange?

"What is it?" David managed weakly. But he knew he had been caught.

"We might not be able to do anything, but someone could." Brandon's voice was strong and sure.

David became confused. "What?"

Amanda looked to David, but then regarded her husband once more. "What are you thinking?"

"Seems to me that if Sadie's mother's state of mind is in question, so will the house and land be. Perhaps she could use someone that knows something about the law."

Brandon couldn't be serious. David was set to leave in six days. The last thing he needed or wanted was further entanglement.

"What do you think, David?" At Brandon's mention of his name, all eyes were on him.

David held up his hands. "I...don't know that this is a good idea. After all, Aunt Sylvia is ready to get back to Richmond. There is much to do to prepare for our trip. I don't know that I have the time to—"

"I think we can make the time," Aunt Sylvia spoke up. "We can't let this innocent girl face down the town on her own, after all."

David frowned. This was not going well.

"Please, David," Amanda said, her eyes glassy with moisture. "At least we can see if she needs legal advice."

That woman was hard to say 'no' to. And while they all looked to him as if he were some sort of savior, which he didn't exactly dislike, he wasn't certain this was his due. Could he offer the advice and still be out of here in six days?

It was true that he didn't like the idea of that lovely woman being pushed around by those misusing the law for their own purposes. The thought of her becoming indigent caused something to rise up in him.

Perhaps he could take a couple of hours to be the hero. Again.

CHAPTER 5
The Offer

"Miss Sadie."

A voice cut through the fog of Sadie's dream. Who was it? It seemed as if the words came from a great distance.

"Miss Sadie, are you well?"

The sound became clearer. Sadie thought that she might should open her eyes, but her eyelids weighed so much. How would she keep them open?

She did manage to lift her lids. And then blinked. The world was blurry.

But as she continued to force her eyes open and shut, her surroundings cleared. She was in her room. And it was light out. Indeed, the sunshine assaulted her senses.

She narrowed her gaze, pulling back from the brightness.

"Miss Sadie?" The voice seemed concerned.

"What?" Sadie rose to a sitting position. Rubbing a hand across her eyes, she welcomed the greater clarity.

Mrs. Wallem stood at her door. At first her form was all Sadie could see. As she focused, however, she could discern the woman's features. And they betrayed Mrs. Wallem's worry, drawn as they were.

"Are you ill?" The words were gentle.

31

Sadie swayed a moment, taking stock of her body. "No. I am well enough. Just tired."

"I'll say that's true."

Then Sadie remembered. Mother has been up most of the night—agitated and roaming. How Sadie hated to use the laudanum Doctor Norwood had entrusted to them. But as morning had neared, Sadie had once again been left without options.

"H-how is Mother?" There must be some reason Mrs. Wallem disturbed Sadie's rest. Was something amiss? Had Mother awakened despite the medicinals?

"She is fine. Still sleeping."

As Sadie should be.

"What..." Sadie swallowed before continuing, "What do you need of me?" She tried to keep her voice free of the frustration pouring through her. At length, she met Mrs. Wallem's gaze.

"You have visitors." The older woman lowered her voice.

"I..." Sadie considered who it might be and if she had the courage to face anyone. "I am not sure I am ready to receive."

"I tried to send them away, but they are insistent." Mrs. Wallem cut her gaze toward the hall.

"Who is it?" Sadie slid off the bed. She must be a sight, having slept in her clothes from yesterday without even bothering to take her hair down.

"Brandon and Amanda Miller. And one of their relatives, I believe."

Sadie stumbled to the vanity. Sleep was not letting go without a fight. She looked at her reflection. Just as she had feared—nothing about her appearance was redeeming. Even her face showed evidence of the long night. The urge to insist the Millers just go away was strong. But Mrs. Miller had always been good to her. Sadie didn't want to be rude.

"Are they in the parlor?" As Sadie's mind continued to clear, she found herself more able to think...more and more with every minute that passed.

"Yes, miss."

"Can you assist me? I think this dress will have to be pressed."

Mrs. Wallem closed the door and moved to Sadie. "Yes. We'll get you out of that and into something else."

They worked together and in a matter of minutes, Sadie stood at the washbowl. She freshened her face and then Mrs. Wallem helped her get redressed. They then joined forces to manage her hair.

As much as Sadie hated to keep her company waiting while she tended to these things, she was much relieved when Mrs. Wallem stepped back and smiled.

"Passable?" Sadie bit at her lower lip. Though whether or not she was presentable, she needed to go and greet her guests.

"More than that, Miss Sadie. I am amazed. You look refreshed. Though I know you can't have rested enough to feel so."

Sadie nodded. Her appearance was nowhere near what it could be. It hadn't been since the incident. Although, she did look surprisingly well put together. They had performed a miracle.

She sighed. "I suppose I'm as ready as I can be."

Mrs. Wallem nodded and moved across the room. She opened the door and lifted a hand in the direction of the hallway.

Gathering what courage she could muster, Sadie rose and walked into the hall.

The parlor was not far—downstairs and to the right. Sadie heard voices long before her feet settled at the base of the stairs. Amanda Miller's was easily recognized. As well as Mr. Miller's. But the other voice—masculine—there was something familiar about it. Was it a ranch hand? No, Mrs. Wallem would have mentioned that. The older woman had not known whomever accompanied the Millers.

Pressing onward, Sadie turned the corner and entered the grand room.

The men stood. Soon after, Mrs. Miller did as well.

Sadie looked down out of habit. It had not always been that way. But the last week had trained her to do so.

"Sadie," Mrs. Miller said as she strode across the room. "How are you?"

Gentle fingers touched Sadie's arm, causing her to look up.

"I'm...as well as I can be." There was no reason to lie. Not anymore.

And though she expected pity to shine through Mrs. Miller's eyes, there was only concern. Could it be that this woman...no more than an acquaintance to her...cared?

"Please, sit, Mrs. Miller," Sadie encouraged. But it was Mrs. Miller who steered Sadie to a settee.

"Call me Amanda. We came because Cook prepared a fine meal for you and your mother."

"That is so...kind." Sadie kept her words short as her throat started to ache. Where were her friends? The ones that she had thought would stay by her no matter what? They had disappeared. And this woman, who she barely knew, had extended grace and generosity.

"I...we...want to make sure you are well. I must apologize, though. We should have come sooner." Was that regret in the woman's voice? How was that possible? Sadie was little more than a stranger to her.

"No," Sadie said as her eyes found Amanda's. "I couldn't be more touched by your gesture." Then Sadie let her gaze move over the men. Something struck her about the other gentleman, the one standing beside Mr. Miller with a markedly taller build and much darker hair. She had seen him before...but where?

Mr. Miller cleared his throat. "Miss Perkins, let me introduce my cousin, David Anderson."

The man moved closer, hand extended.

It was the man from yesterday—the stranger who came to her aid.

"I know you." Sadie gasped as she slid a hand into his. "From the telegraph office." Why had it taken her so long to remember? He had been rather thoughtful yesterday. And his protective nature had made her pause. For at last, someone saw her. And cared.

"Yes." Mr. Anderson glanced at the Millers as he licked his lips. "I believe I did come across you."

"You did much more than that, Mr. Anderson." She choked back her rising emotions yet again. "Your assistance was..." What was the word?

"It was nothing, miss." His voice warmed her senses.

Only then did she realize, he still held her hand. She tugged it free as her face heated.

"David is in town, visiting," Mr. Miller said, looking from Sadie to David and back.

"Ah. I see." Sadie glanced down at her hands by her waist, and she fingered the gathered pleats of the skirt. So, he wasn't here to stay. Just one more person who would leave her.

Stop that, she admonished herself. He didn't owe her anything. Though he *had* inserted himself into the situation when she'd needed him. That was all. It wasn't as if he was abandoning her.

She peered up to see Mr. Miller exchange a look with Amanda and then nudge Mr. Anderson with his shoulder. What was that about?

Amanda touched Sadie's forearm. "We want to help in any way we can."

"I thank you." But could anyone truly help her? In a way that mattered? The food was a kindness to be sure, but she was in a hopeless situation.

"I...understand that your mother is rather...ill." Amanda's words were measured, chosen carefully.

Sadie shot her a look. What did she know? What could she know? Had Mrs. Wallem been loose-lipped?

"Not to worry," Amanda was quick to say. "We don't intend to make that common knowledge."

What was their real purpose in coming here? This seemed to be more than a social call.

"I...am a lawyer." Mr. Anderson's words were tentative. As if he wasn't sure about something.

"Oh?" Sadie wasn't certain what he was getting at. The shock of Amanda's words—that revelation—still flowed over her. She couldn't get a handle on what it might mean for her mother should her condition be known outside of these walls.

"And I," Mr. Anderson said, looking to Mr. Miller for a moment before settling his gaze back on her, "Would like to offer you whatever assistance I can."

He wanted to help her? How? Sadie couldn't make sense of all the information coming at her. If only she'd had more rest. "Whatever assistance you can?"

Amanda leaned forward. "We want you to know you're not alone. David can give you advice about your mother's situation—perhaps explore your options."

It hit Sadie. Was Mr. Anderson offering to take up her case for

Mother's sanity? Wasn't it best to simply hide it? "I'm not sure I should push the issue."

"Miss Perkins, if I may be so bold," Mr. Anderson began. He stepped closer and continued, "Your mother's situation will not remain a secret for long. She, and you, will need someone with legal knowledge. Perhaps if we can establish a guardianship, that might afford her and the estate some protection."

Not as much as marrying Josiah would have. Sadie sighed even as her chest tightened. But there was a glimmer of hope stirring in her at Mr. Anderson's words. Did he truly intend to help her make a way through this mess?

Sadie glanced between the three, tears building. She blinked hard against them. "I...don't know what to say."

"Don't be quick with thanks yet." Mr. Anderson leaned away. "I'm not certain what can be done. But I promise, I will do everything within legal reach.

Sadie nodded. That was fair, though the non-committal tone gnawed at her. Still, this was the best she could hope for. And she would take it.

She stood. Surprise registered on their faces around her. But she focused on Mr. Miller's cousin. "I thank you, Mr. Anderson. Your offer is more than I dare ask. Of anyone. And I will pay you for your services."

He shifted his weight from his left foot to his right. "That's not necessary, I—"

"I insist." She would not be beholden to another man. "It may not be what you are used to, but I will pay what I can. Does that suit you?"

The corners of his mouth lifted as if he found something about her stubbornness to admire. "I look forward to it."

And that...was that.

David couldn't help but smile as he, Brandon, and Amanda waved farewell to Sadie. Nor could he deny that the urge to look back once more was irresistible. Indeed, he did glance over his shoulder. She stood at the door, watching them. He offered her one more of his charming grins.

It had felt good to step in. And her reaction, though strange at first, was as it should be. She was grateful. He had indeed been the hero this day.

Now for the hard work of putting in the research, paperwork, and time to figure out if this mess could be sorted. But if anyone could, he would.

"You coming?" Brandon called from some distance ahead.

David stumbled as he jerked his head back in the direction he walked. He hadn't meant to stare. But Sadie had stepped within and closed the door. Perhaps she didn't see his embarrassing misstep.

"Whoa, there." Brandon's words came on a chuckle. What was he thinking about David's lapse?

"I'm coming," David assured his cousin. "Just making sure Miss Perkins was safely within."

Brandon smirked. Must he?

Likely, his cousin thought more of this than he ought. The last thing David wanted, or needed, was to get involved any further than offering legal services. With any luck, he'd still be out of here on schedule.

Something tugged at him, warning that he had committed to more than that. But he pushed it aside. He would be on that train come Wednesday. Whatever it took.

Brandon had turned and was helping his wife into the wagon.

David grumbled. Yet another dusty ride through the wilds of Arizona.

Still, he offered Amanda a tight smile as he climbed onto the back bench. At least he'd have her company to distract from Brandon's lack of conversation and, maybe worse, his possible insinuations.

"It really is good of you," Amanda said, sniffling. Not this again.

"Nothing to it." But David's chest swelled all the same. Not only was he stepping in to save the day, but his humble service was also gaining him Amanda's admiration.

"But it is," Amanda insisted. "To her, it might mean everything."

Yes, he was aware. That didn't mean he had to gloat. But a little pride in his selflessness was warranted. And as he mulled on that, Brandon and Amanda chatted. Their voices were aimed at each other, and their tones were rather muted. Obviously, it was a conversation he was not invited into. No matter, his thoughts turned to Sadie.

Mrs. Perkins, of questionable sanity, had been left with little to stand on. And Sadie had no more rights to the property and whatever monies remained than her mother. Many factors loomed, begging to be uncovered. Did the property belong solely to the double-crossing Mr. Perkins? Or was Mrs. Perkins the recipient of an inheritance apart from her marital assets? That might place these things in her care regardless. He chased his thoughts for a few moments, the legal ramifications of various situations tumbling as well. Until he reached an impasse. He needed more information. That would either make their case for them or eliminate Sadie and her mother's chances altogether.

He shifted. His body wearied of the constant bumping.

"You all right?" Amanda asked.

He caught her eyes. How long had she been watching him?

"Yes, just thinking." He dipped his head in her direction.

"I'm glad to hear it." She then turned and focused on her husband once more, winding an arm through his.

Once again, David marveled at the picture the couple made and the ache that it brought. Claire's rejection a few month's past still stung. But could he ever have had with her what Brandon and his Amanda did? He wasn't sure. And that hurt more. All the time, effort, and emotion spent on courtship...only to have it come to naught.

The wagon slowed. They approached the ranch. How had the time passed so quickly? He must have been very deep in thought. All the better. He did so tire of these rustic landscapes.

As they neared the barn, David spotted two of the ranch hands. Again, no names to go with the faces. The two men appeared caught up in a rather heated discussion.

Brandon's shoulders straightened and his muscles tensed. What was going on here?

The cart came to a rather abrupt halt as Brandon jerked the reins before dropping down and leaving the horse in Amanda's care.

"What exactly does he plan to do?" David wondered aloud.

"He'll try to break this up. If he can." Amanda's words seemed wishful. Were these rough men usually like this?

David dropped his leg over the side.

"What are you doing?" Amanda's tone did not hold her typical gentleness.

"I'm going to help."

Her mouth opened.

David cut her off. "I'm not about to sit here and watch these men tear into each other like a couple of barbarians." He jumped down and moved toward the ruffians without giving Amanda space to speak further.

As David neared the small cluster, Brandon's voice rose. The ranch hands did not take their eyes off each other. Or slacken their tension. This was not going well. Why wouldn't Brandon slip in between them? That would certainly diffuse the situation.

David paused as he reached Brandon. His last words were all David caught.

"...run my ranch."

Oh, bother. Why would he make this about him?

David took another step.

Brandon gripped his arm. "What are you doing?" Did he intend to hold David back?

"Trying to stop this before it goes any further." David set his hardest gaze on Brandon. Then he shook off his cousin's hand.

"I wouldn't..." Brandon warned.

But that wasn't something David couldn't have guessed. Of course, Brandon wouldn't step in. That's why he failed to put these men in their place.

"Listen, gentlemen," David said as he came closer.

Narrowed gazes flitted to him. Good. He had their attention.

"Now, then, let's settle this like men. Not like animals."

"He's nothing but a liar," the taller ranch hand seethed.

David dared another step. "I'm sure it might seem that way, but we can come to an understanding if you'll just—"

"A liar, am I?" the other man yelled.

A fist flew. David didn't have time to think. A second later, his face exploded with pain, and he fell back. But he didn't hit the ground.

Brandon braced him. "I told you to—"

"You hit me!" David yelled at the man. "Why did you hit me?"

The two backed away from each other and glared at David. Neither showed any remorse.

"You are just overgrown boys." David's head swam. Something wasn't right about his vision. The world tilted.

"What did you say?" It was the taller ranch hand.

Brandon shoved David back and stood between him and the angered ranch hands. "That's quite enough. You," he said, pointing to the stockier man, "to the bunkhouse. And you..." He jabbed a finger at the other one. "To the homestead. You both need to cool off."

As if that would work. It was all David could do to not scoff.

Yet, after one more exchanged glare, the men spun and marched to their separate spaces.

"Are you all right?" Amanda called. The swish of skirts gave away that she neared them.

David felt as if his eye would pop out of his face. He touched along his eyebrow on that side of his face, tenderly testing the skin underneath as well as checking his nose. Nothing seemed broken or bleeding.

He noticed that Brandon wouldn't look at him. His cousin's gaze was trained on the pasture. At length, he spoke. "You need to be more mindful of—"

"And maybe you should have a better handle on your men." David shot back. Maybe it was harsh, but he couldn't quell the anger rising within.

"Now don't you two start." Amanda's voice was rougher than he'd ever heard it.

"I'm going to get cleaned up." David turned and moved off in the direction of the homestead.

This was exactly what he got for trying to help—nothing but pain and injury. He couldn't stop his thoughts from wandering to Sadie. Where would his offer to help her lead?

CHAPTER 6
News

Mrs. Wallem moved through the house. Or at least Sadie hoped it was the older housekeeper. For Sadie hadn't the capacity to address any more situations with Mother right now. When would things calm down? Ever?

Sadie stepped out into the hall and looked to the right and left. Sure enough, Mrs. Wallem came around the corner. The woman looked both worn and exhausted.

Sadie could certainly relate.

These last several days had become progressively worse. How would they survive if Aunt Jane wasn't able to help? It was Sadie's last hope. There was no other recourse if Aunt Jane couldn't come.

Would that mean Mother would end up in one of those sanitariums? A ward of some kind? Sadie couldn't bear the thought of it. No, that would not do. She could never subject her mother to such. Did she have a choice though?

Yes, she did. And as long as she did, she would take it.

"Mrs. Wallem," she began. How she hated what she would have to ask! But she had to. "I need to make a short trip into town to check the post."

The woman's tired eyes widened with understanding. She, too, must know that this was their only salvation. At length, she nodded.

Sadie slipped back into her room.

Mrs. Wallem followed. "You need to stop and see Dr. Norwood to secure more of that medicine."

Sadie shut her eyes. Had they gone through their supply so fast? How could they continue at this rate?

But she pressed the hardness out of her features as she turned and reached for the woman's hand. "I will."

No matter what it took. This was the only way.

Sadie gathered the rest of the things she needed. "I will be back shortly."

Then, without chancing a potentially discouraging glance at the woman who was her only ally, she stepped out the door and toward her horse.

The ride to town was short and labored. She needed Aunt Jane's answer to have arrived, and for her mother's relative to be here soon after it.

She steered her horse up to the telegraph office then slid off.

The eyes of everyone in the immediate area were on her. No doubt judging her. Why must they? Sadie tired of the scrutiny.

What, after all, was their obsession? Did their lives contain so little excitement? But she knew the truth—it was a small town with little else to occupy the residents but these bits of drama. Where were the days when everyone was so fixated on work and survival that they didn't have the time for such stuff and nonsense?

She pushed past the glares and moved toward the office.

As she neared the door, a figure stepped out. It was difficult to keep from bumping into the woman.

"My apologies!" Sadie gripped the doorframe, thankful she had not knocked the woman down.

"Goodness! As well you should be." The woman had a hand over her heart. "You walk about as if you own the place. Frightening the good people of this town!"

"I am sorry, ma'am." She reached out a hand. "If there is anything I can—"

The woman jerked away as if afraid she'd be stung. "No! For goodness sake's no!" She side-stepped Sadie and moved off, head high, not offering so much as a backward look over her shoulder.

Sadie's heart dropped. It was not, then, as if this animosity was imagined. This *was* what they thought of her. What had she done to make her neighbors and friends think so ill?

Slinking through the doorway, she didn't look up until she was in the middle of the office.

The line that typically filled the small establishment was not present. At least that was some bit of grace in this life.

Sadie stepped to the counter, trying to keep her hopes in check. She wiped at her brow, smoothing her hair back into place. "Do you have anything for me?"

"Yes, I..." the telegraph operator said as he looked about the small stacks on the counter. "A telegram just came for you. Ah...here it is."

Sadie tried to suppress emotions that bubbled up. The last thing she wanted was to give the townsfolk more to wag their tongues about.

The man set a paper on the counter.

Sadie tried not to look up, but she couldn't help herself.

The telegraph operator offered a small smile but did not let his lips lift any higher into a true grin. In fact, his mouth dropped almost as soon as the gesture could be noticed. "Do you need anything else, miss?"

She shook her head even as she reached for the paper.

Dare she read it? Would it seal her fate? Or rather...her mother's?

Taking the thin paper, she tucked it close to her chest. Should she read it here or wait? Where would she go? She didn't want an audience, but she certainly couldn't hold off until she got back to the house.

She peered down at the telegram but couldn't make herself read it. What if Aunt Jane said no? Could she bear it? Could she contain her emotion? No, it would be best if she waited until she would not become a spectacle.

Sadie swept up her skirt hem and turned, rushing from the office. The solace of the open would be but minutes away once she was on the horse. She slammed into a firm form.

Hands touched her elbows as she chided herself for rushing again—and this time she had slammed into a gentleman.

She jerked away. "Sir, pardon me!" Her face burned. How could she be so careless...twice! "I am—"

"It is nothing." The voice had a kind lilt. Comforting. Soothing almost.

She peered up into the face of David Anderson.

"Are you quite all right?" He eased her body away from his.

"I...think so." She looked down at the space between them. They were so close; it should feel intrusive. Yet it did not. Was she so starved for human contact?

"Please, let me help you to sit for a minute. Are you certain you are uninjured?" He gripped her elbow and led her farther into the office, to a bench within.

The telegraph operator threw a glance in their direction, shook his head, and went about his work.

Yes, she was ridiculous. Most certainly so.

Even as she settled onto the seat at Mr. Anderson's behest, she tried to hide her face. But why? That seemed a bit rude...and unnecessary.

"You are certain you are well?" The man's eyes shone the concern emanating from him.

How was it possible that someone she'd only met a few days ago would have such compassion? Truly he must be a good man.

"What is this?" he indicated the paper she still clutched.

"This?" She lifted it slightly, but once again couldn't make herself read it. "A telegram."

"Pardon. I didn't mean to intrude." He looked away.

She set a hand to his arm. "No, it's fine. It's just..." Why was she willing to share something so private with this man? What was it about him that disarmed her so?

His eyes met hers. They were dark and curious. She trusted him. Perhaps more than she should.

Sadie settled the paper, and her hands, in her lap. "I sent off to my aunt for help. These last several days, things have been...difficult." She chanced a glance at his eyes once more and wanted to melt from the intensity of his interest. How long had it been since someone saw her... really saw her?

"I'm sorry to hear that." His voice was warm.

She believed him. But it wasn't about that. He didn't want to hear about her troubles.

"What did she say?" His question was not prying, but more... considerate.

Her face heated. How could she explain? But his care for her situation banished her trepidation. "I...haven't read it."

"No?" His eyes widened slightly, and he seemed to be taking her in.

"I was...worried. And so, I just couldn't bring myself to read it. Not yet." She pressed out a breath and peered down at the crinkled parchment. And then an idea struck her. Could she ask it of him? Was it too personal? But the words were out before she could stop them. "Would you read it for me?"

He pulled back just a bit. "Me? You want me to read your aunt's correspondence?"

She knew she did want that. The news would be so much better coming from him rather than sterile letters.

His eyebrow piqued as he regarded her. "You are certain?"

She nodded. "Please?" Holding out the paper, she fought to keep her fingers from trembling.

He enveloped her hand and the tremors stopped. "Of course."

Though he only held her hand, she felt as if he had drawn her into some space that was outside of this place. That they existed and nothing else. If his touch on her hand could do this, what might it be like to be in his arms?

She swallowed as she pushed down that thought. Such was not an appropriate thing to think of someone she had just met.

He slid the parchment from her hand but held her eyes. Was he as mesmerized by this moment as she was?

At length, he tore his gaze from hers and looked at the telegram.

She held her breath.

He sighed and met her eyes again. "She's coming."

"Truly?" Sadie gasped.

He nodded and maneuvered so she could look at the paper as well. There it was in plain script: *I will arrive on the train next week.*

Aunt Jane would come? Overwhelming relief rippled through

Sadie. She felt lighter than she had in months. There was hope! Turning, she embraced the man who had shown her such kindness.

"I can't believe it! This is great news!" She worked to contain her tears.

His arms came around her, and he held her loosely.

A moment later, she realized what she had done. And disentangled herself from him. Her features burned.

"Mr. Anderson, I am so sorry. I don't know what came over me."

His hand still lay on her arm. "No need to apologize." He then released her and straightened his jacket. And he looked toward the back of the office.

The telegraph operator! He must have seen the whole exchange.

Sadie wished she could disappear right then and there. More gossip that would further tarnish her was the last thing she needed.

David watched Sadie's delicate features as she looked down. Her cheeks reddened and her countenance dropped. Why was that? True, he had been surprised by her embrace, but was it so terrible?

He reached out a hand toward her arm but held himself back. This didn't seem the right moment to press the issue. Becoming acutely aware of eyes on him, he looked past Sadie.

The telegraph operator glared at the two of them for a moment longer before returning to his work, shaking his head.

Did the man think there was something inappropriate going on between he and Miss Perkins? David swallowed. Nothing could be further from the truth, but how was he to express that?

Glancing back at Sadie, whose gaze was still set on the floorboards, David cleared his throat.

That got her attention. She peered at him.

"I...am so pleased your aunt is coming," he offered, trying to calm his breathing.

Sadie nodded with some hesitation. The lightness that had filled her before had disappeared. And it made him sad.

Had he enjoyed having her in his arms? Perhaps more than he

should? He wished he could tamp down whatever this was in him... whatever filled him when he was around her. Surely it was nothing more than attraction to a beautiful woman. Yes, that must be it. For he had determined no woman would ever gain his affection. He would not find himself at the mercy of another. Being played a fool once was enough. Perhaps this plan to assist Sadie with her legal challenges was not wise, considering these feelings.

"I'm sure you need to be on your way." Sadie's voice sounded so small. It made him ache. "I...won't keep you any longer."

"No," he said a bit faster than he'd intended. "That is, I'm not in any rush. Might I walk you to your cart? Or see you safely home?"

She played with her fingers in her lap; the telegram in her grip became even more crumpled. "I appreciate your kindness, sir. But I am not headed home just yet."

"Oh? You have other business in town?" He set his hands on his knees. That may help him keep the defiant limbs from reaching out again.

She nodded and the slightest smile graced her lips.

He watched her expression for any hint that he intruded.

But there was no semblance of hurry about her, or sense that she found him intrusive. But he wondered if he did, in fact, keep her from her errand. After some moments, he realized that he stared at her.

"Forgive me," he said as he stood. There, that was better. Remove himself from temptation altogether. "I did not mean to stare...that is..." He paused, taking a breath, and chiding himself for the slip of tongue. "I did not intend to keep *you*."

Sadie rose as well. "I truly appreciate your kindness, Mr. Anderson."

He nodded as he ushered her toward the door, being mindful to keep a good two inches between his hand and her back. "Please, call me David."

They were now outside the small office, the sun beating down on them, and the smell of the kicked up dust assaulting his senses.

Her head was down again. "Thank you...David. You made a difficult situation bearable."

He lowered his gaze to try and catch her eye. It did not escape his notice that the few townsfolk in the vicinity fairly glowered at her. His chest tightened, and he felt the need to wrap her in his arms once more —to protect and shield her somehow.

"Good day, Mr. Anderson—er, David." She glanced up at him and offered a sweet smile.

It nearly undid him. His hand shot out as if of its own accord and set upon her arm. "Shall I walk you?" Where did that come from?

"I..." She looked down the main stretch.

That had been rather impertinent of him. How was he to know whether her business might be of a personal nature?

Indecision flashed across her face, and she glanced about at the people passing by. Those whose opinion he cared naught for. Her uncertainty faded and her eyes cleared. "I would like that."

His heart thumped hard in response. "Very well then."

With some awkwardness about her, she turned to the right and walked on.

He let his hand drop and picked up his pace to stay in step with her. For some minutes, there was no conversation between them. What was there to say? He didn't really know her. But there was something about being in her presence that brought every one of his nerve endings to life.

"What finds you in Wharton City today?" she asked.

"I came to check the post."

She paused. "Oh...I apologize."

Apologize? For what? Then he realized—bumping into her had distracted him from his own errand. He shook his head. "No need. I will attend to that later. There is nothing pressing I am expecting."

Her features softened. Almost in a sad way.

He reran his words...why did he have to make it sound as if he only escorted her for lack of anything better? That if he had sought something more interesting, he would not have joined her?

"Besides," he tried again, "I rather enjoy the distraction."

Distraction? Was that all she was? He wanted to kick himself. Where was his mind? Why did his tongue insist on running away?

"I see." She seemed rather intent on the walkway in front of her.

This was coming out all wrong. But he couldn't think of how to repair his misstep.

Sadie slowed. Was something amiss? David turned to investigate.

"This is...that is, my business is with Dr. Norwood." She was once again the timid creature he had seen most often. Where was the lively woman he had but glimpsed? And how could he encourage that out of her? Had her circumstances so beaten her down?

Her face had a pink hue about it. Why would that be?

And he caught himself. She must want to extricate herself from him but didn't wish to share more than necessary.

"I thank you for the fine walk, Miss Perkins," he said.

"Call me Sadie." Her features warmed as if a testament to her sincerity.

"Sadie." He let her name fall from his lips. It felt good.

"Thank you again...for your assistance." She offered him a smile.

"Of course." He shifted his weight and tried to decide how to end this interaction without it being abrupt or lingering.

With a quick nod of her head, Sadie turned.

Now that had been more awkward than he'd planned. How could he not command himself better than this?

"Sadie," he said, reaching a hand out to touch her arm.

She turned.

"Please, do let me know if there is ever anything I can do." He glanced around them. "I..."

The door to the clinic opened and Dr. Norwood stepped out. "Hello, there, Miss Perkins. I didn't quite expect to see you today." Then the doctor settled his gaze on David. "How can I help you two?"

"Oh," Sadie said, that adorable pink coloring her features again. "We aren't...that is, *I* came to see you."

David wished he could just sink into the planked sidewalk. How had he managed to get himself into such an embarrassing situation? "Please," he spoke up, "Don't mind me. I was just wishing Sadie—Miss Perkins a fine day."

The doctor cocked his head to the side as he continued to examine the two of them.

Sadie wouldn't so much as glance in David's direction. Was she so ashamed? Or was there something more to her behavior?

"Good day, Miss Perkins." He bowed his head slightly.

She looked at his feet and nodded as well. "Good day, Mr. Anderson."

With that, he turned and walked back in the direction they had come. He *did*, after all, need to check the post and be on his way. But the stirring in his chest gave him pause. What was he getting himself into with this woman? He'd best keep his distance. There was no room for error...or for him to become too entangled with a local girl. No, he was determined he would be saying farewell to Wharton City for good in a matter of days.

CHAPTER 7
Unsettled

D avid stared at himself in the mirror. The distant clanging of breakfast dishes being moved and washed scattered his concentration. Though he was dashing...for certain. He turned his chin upward and to the right, admiring his freshly shaved jawline. If only everyone in this rustic place could have such fine hygiene habits.

A loud crash sounded, and he dropped the mirror.

Did the women have to be so noisy? Between the dishes and the talking, it was impossible to think. It was bad enough that Aunt Sylvia stooped so low as to help with these kitchen tasks that were best left to the help. But they paid him no mind on this subject.

Picking up the mirror, he looked for any hint the ornate piece had cracked. He breathed a sigh. There was nothing amiss.

As he jerked on the lapels of his jacket, he gathered his wits about him. He would need them today. If he was going to bring this obligation to a close.

Was that what he wanted? To finish his business with Sadie this day and say a final farewell to the becoming lady?

He shook his head. It didn't matter how his deceptive heart tugged at him; he would not succumb. There was a train leaving on Wednesday. And he would be on it. That was final.

Letting out a breath, he grabbed his case and stepped out of the room. As he moved through the house, he was now thankful for the clattering of pots. It would divert the womenfolk from any sound he might make on his way out of the house.

Indeed, he was undisturbed as he stepped onto the porch. He drew in a breath. His gaze drifted over the pastureland and to the horizon. It was expansive. Enough room for a man to get lost.

That was not to be his fate, however. His life was set. On the right trajectory—upward. Though he couldn't help but envy his cousin just a little. For this land that didn't seem as atrocious as when David had first arrived, and for the wife that loved Brandon so completely.

David shook his head. There was no sense in bemoaning that. He had made his decision in those regards. And he was set in it. He would not become romantically attached. Not again. The resulting weakness should he let himself fall under another woman's spell could not be tolerated. And it would not be.

Creaking on the steps drew his attention. One of the ranch hands, the only one that had not been involved in the fight the other day, came closer.

David tipped his head in greeting as he maneuvered to go around the man.

"Mr. Anderson," the baby-faced man said, halting just short of David.

David arched a brow. "What can I do for you?"

"Mr. Miller sent me. He said you are planning to head into town today."

"Yes, I am." Not that it was any of this youngster's business. "I have an appointment to keep." Yes, an appointment. That was, after all, what this meeting with Sadie was. Business.

"Junior needs the wagon for an errand to the General Store."

"Junior?" Which one was that again? He prayed it wasn't the man who had struck him.

"Yeah. We need some feed. Just wanted to let you know so you can catch a ride with him." The simple man before him turned.

David had no choice but to follow. They made their way to the barn where, sure enough, the oaf who had punched him worked to ready the cart. There was absolutely no way on this earth David would get in the cart with this man.

He reached out and tapped the ranch hand near him. "Where is Brandon—er, Mr. Miller?"

The man-child made a partial turn and pointed across to the side paddock. Indeed, David spotted Brandon within the enclosed area, working one of the horses.

Frowning, David nodded his thanks to the lad, stepped past the cart, and to the fence. "Brandon," he called.

His cousin did not acknowledge him. Because he didn't hear? Or because he avoided David?

"Brandon," he said a bit louder.

That brought some semblance of awareness. Brandon jerked his head in David's direction. He held a finger up. Must David wait while Brandon finished his task? He pushed out a breath. This was tiresome.

As he watched, Brandon did something with the horse's back hooves. It looked utterly disgusting. Who knew what that horse had stepped in? Especially in this yard. He looked around and could not help the gag that rose in his throat at the sight. But he resisted the impulse and looked away.

Soon enough the horse moved off and David looked up. Brandon took off his gloves and walked to the fence. Thank the Lord he had worn protection for his hands. Not that it mattered, his hands had so many callouses already.

"What can I do for you?" Brandon asked, rubbing a bandana across his forehead. The days had become more heated of late. Each one more so than the last.

David squared his shoulders. "I have an appointment with Miss Perkins today."

"Yes, I am aware. Junior is hitching the wagon." Brandon's brow furrowed as if confused by David's words.

"That man..." David calmed himself. There was no benefit in letting his voice rise and his emotions rule him. "Lest you forgot, he struck me. I have no intention of riding into town with him." He knew he sounded weak. And petty. But he didn't care. What would the man do if he became frustrated with David? Or just wanted to get another hit in?

Brandon set one booted foot onto the lowest slat of the fencing and looked off toward the cart. Then back at David. "We only have the one wagon."

David straightened his posture and tugged at his jacket. "I understand. Is it not possible for one of the other ranch hands to take me?"

Brandon shook his head.

Why? David bemoaned. *Why do these things happen to me?*

"There is one other option I can offer." Brandon eased back.

"Yes? Anything!" David avoided Brandon's gaze. He hadn't intended to be so quick or so adamant.

"You could take the painted mare." Brandon jerked his head toward the animal in the paddock with him.

"I could...what?" Did Brandon really think he would ride upon that filthy animal? It wasn't that he hadn't learned to ride. But only out of necessity. Horses were smelly and dirty. Horseback was most certainly not his preferred method of travel. How would it be for him to show up to Sadie's house with the stench of the animal upon him? Could he bear it?

"Those are the only options I can offer you. Junior needs the cart to get feed for the horses, and the other ranch hands are busy. Your choice." Brandon pushed away from the fence and stepped to the wooden trough.

"All right," David shot out. "I'll take the horse."

Brandon gave him a sideways glance. "You sure?"

"Yes." *Bless it all!* David sighed. He had been backed into a corner.

Brandon nodded. "I'll get her saddled."

David stepped toward the barn. And then, as an afterthought, called out to his cousin who had already made his way to the horse. "Thanks."

Why did Brandon look so shocked? It wasn't as if David lacked proper manners. Just one more thing to ensure this place was not endearing to him.

Why today? Sadie ran a hand over the stiff fabric of her fine dress. Why must all of her clothing be so confining and fanciful? It wasn't as if she lived the same life she had a month ago.

Mother had been especially difficult this morning. Mrs. Wallem had needed to dose her...again. These episodes were longer and more frequent and more difficult to bring to an end. What would that mean in a week? A month? Lord willing, a year?

Sadie couldn't bear that thought. It was just too exhausting and depressing. She put away the remaining morning dishes. What would her father think of her now? Doing menial labor to care for the house? He would be aghast. But it couldn't be helped. Mrs. Wallem could not maintain everything and assist with Mother. She decided she cared not for her father's opinion on the matter. After all, wasn't it his fault? If he hadn't abandoned them, they'd still have a full staff. It wouldn't all be left to her and Mrs. Wallem.

Closing her eyes, Sadie sent up a prayer for perseverance. These moments and simple prayers were the only things sustaining her.

The gentle rumble of trotting hooves drew her attention to the window. There, in the distance, a figure upon a horse approached. For whatever reason, she had expected David to come by way of cart. Why... she wasn't certain. She just did.

Straightening her dress, she moved out of the kitchen and toward the front door. Why had she told him they could meet here? Ah yes, because she hadn't wanted prying eyes and eavesdropping ears from the townspeople. But now she dreaded him coming here and the risk that he might hear or see Mother. What would he do? Insist that she be put in an asylum? Report the situation himself?

A shiver ran down Sadie's spine. He had seemed kind enough the few times she had been with him. Why think otherwise now?

It was all in her head...her fear.

Regardless, it was best they keep Mother tucked away while he was here. They had to.

Just as the hoofbeats came to a halt, Sadie took a breath and counted to ten. Then she opened the door.

David was beside the horse, unclipping his bag from the saddle. He did not appear to be as comfortable with the animal. Every time the mare shifted, he jerked back. It was almost comical. Indeed, Sadie probably would have laughed if not for her heavy apprehension.

"Good morning, Mr. Anderson!" she called.

He whirled toward where she stood just within the door frame. Then he brushed his hair back and offered a smile. "Good morning, Miss Perkins."

Was he so surprised? Maybe he expected her to be seated comfortably in her room or the parlor awaiting Mrs. Wallem to bring her guest in. Such was no longer the formality she could afford.

Still, her heart dropped at the realization of how she must appear to such a fine gentleman. One whose opinion mattered more than perhaps it should.

David strolled to the door as he brushed at his jacket. He looked immaculate. What was he dusting off?

She bit at her lip. Could she suggest they go to the café in town perhaps? That would likely seem rather strange. It may be best to trust the Lord's provision of laudanum and let him within.

He stepped closer, pausing just short of where she stood. His eyes were intent on hers. "How are you today, Sadie?"

The ease in which her name fell from his mouth caused something to spark within her. Was this a hint that she might have another ally? But how much could she trust him? She had trusted Josiah, and that had not ended well.

Turning her face upward, she smiled. "I am well enough. And you?"

She cringed within at the pleasantries. Sadie both missed and loathed them. They seemed pointless here. But she had not been spoken to so kindly by a man in some time.

"I...cannot complain." He offered a smile. Why did he have to be so charming?

She became aware of the fact that they stood, facing off at the doorway to the house. "Please, do come in," she said as she opened the door wider and moved to the side for him to pass.

When he stepped within, his body passing so close to hers, something warm spindled in her chest. Indeed, she was too starved for human contact and kindness.

Shutting the door, she once more smoothed down her skirt before holding up her arm in the direction of the parlor. "This way."

They walked down the hall and she couldn't help but wonder if he radiated heat. For the warmth was now at her back as he followed.

She moved into the parlor and found a seat.

He remained at the doorway, a strange look upon his features. What was his concern? Her reputation? His?

"Mrs. Wallem is just down the hall. She will be able to chaperone."

He nodded and glanced in the direction she had indicated. "We may need to discuss things of a sensitive nature. Will she be able to hear us?"

"Yes." Sadie met his gaze as he turned back to her. "But I trust her implicitly."

He frowned. "Perhaps your mother could chaperone."

"No," Sadie rose, her words coming sharper than she'd intended.

David's eyes widened.

Oh goodness, she had done it again. Let her anxious heart give away more than she'd wanted. "That is, mother is sleeping. It has been...hard for her to sleep since Father left."

Sadie's face warmed. That wasn't exactly a lie. It was, however, more than she'd wished to expose.

David nodded. "I can imagine." He stepped into the parlor and found a seat opposite hers, pulling a notebook out of his bag and settling into the chair.

Sadie sank into her seat once more.

"Now then...I need some basic information."

She nodded. And prayed his questions would not be too prying.

He grabbed a writing instrument from the case as well. "Mostly about your mother..."

Dread fell over her. This was her worst fear come true. He would dig into Mother's situation. What could she do? Refuse to answer? Tell him to leave?

He looked over his notes. "In regards to the property..."

Sadie let out a breath. Maybe she had reacted too quickly. These may very well be benign interrogatives.

"...are they solely your father's?"

"Pardon?"

"How did your father acquire the land, house, and other assets?"

"The property and house were part of an inheritance to my mother. There has been additional work done to the house." She looked around the room, the home she had always lived in.

"So, the property has your mother's name on it as well?" He looked at her, an eyebrow raised.

"I am not sure that I follow." She leaned forward.

"If your mother inherited the property, then there is precedence for her to be able to maintain control of it. Whatever she brought into the marriage can perhaps be ascribed to her care...certainly in your father's absence. Perhaps permanently."

"But I thought..." Sadie paused and swallowed before continuing, "I didn't think that married women could have anything...that didn't really belong to her husband."

David shook his head. "It's not quite so clear cut. The law sometimes isn't. There have been laws passed in Mississippi and New York, to name a couple, that protect the women in these kinds of cases."

Crash.

Something had shattered. Sadie rose. Had Mother awakened?

"Excuse me," she said as she rushed for the door. "I need to check on that."

David stood as well. But she was out of the room and closing the door before he could say anything.

Sadie's heart pounded as she made her way through the hall. And as she neared Mother's room, a screeching became loud enough for her to hear. Even through the strong wooden door between her and Mother. Mrs. Wallem's calming voice was also there. Dare Sadie enter the room and disrupt the goings on? Or should she allow Mrs. Wallem to handle it?

She looked back toward the parlor and to her mother's door. And decided it best she put this to rest soon. Rather than risk David overhearing.

Slipping into the room, she found Mother abed. But the woman was agitated, to say the least. Arms flailing, she fought Mrs. Wallem, who tried to keep Mother settled.

"Get away from me," Mother screamed.

"Don't," Mrs. Wallem's kind voice became harder. "You'll only injure yourself."

Then Sadie saw it—the floor. Mother must have knocked over some sort of glass. The broken pieces littered the floor. She sidestepped the mess on her way to the bed. "Ma, don't fight. You're home. You're safe."

Mrs. Wallem let out a breath. Was it relief for Sadie's presence or frustration?

"Where is the laudanum?" Sadie asked, as she reached for her mother's hands.

Mrs. Wallem jerked her head toward the mess of glass. "She knocked it out of my hands."

Sadie's heart fell. What were they to do without the precious medicine? How could she calm her mother? Or keep this from David? Might Mrs. Wallem be able to hold Mother off long enough for Sadie to dismiss the man?

Mother arched her body and then kicked out. Her foot slammed into Sadie, knocking her to the floor and causing her to fall onto her backside and hands.

A sharp stinging shot through her. She lifted her hands to check them and realized she had fallen into the glass. Blood covered her palms from multiple cuts and abrasions. What was she to do now? How was she to regain her feet?

Mrs. Wallem continued to try and calm Mother, speaking soft and soothing words to her. But Mother was too upset. Too out of sorts.

Sadie wanted to cry, but she dared not. Though as she moved to get up, she struggled to think how to do so.

"What is this?" a male voice came from the direction of the hall.

Everything in Sadie caved in. David stood at the doorway, staring at the scene.

CHAPTER 8
Distraught

David's heart stopped as he looked in the small bedchamber. Sadie was on the floor amidst a smattering of broken glass. The woman in the bed thrashed about. Mrs. Wallem either worked to contain the older woman or she had incited the whole thing. It was difficult to determine. But his eyes were latched on Sadie.

As were hers on him. But her expression read surprise. And perhaps...horror?

He closed the distance between them, careful as he made a path through the jagged pieces. And then he reached for her.

She drew her hands back. Almost protectively.

Then he saw—there were lacerations on her palms. His heart ached at the sight.

Gripping her elbows, he lifted her to stand.

She leaned into him and let out a whimper as she gained her feet. Her dress was smeared with her blood.

He glanced at the two other women in the room. If only he could do something for them. At the very least, he wished he could make sense of what was happening. But now was not the time. Sadie was injured, and she needed attention.

Catching her gaze again, he pulled her toward the door.

She did not fight him. Had he expected her to? He wasn't sure.

Leading her into the hall, he realized that he had no idea where the kitchen might be. Or if that would be the best place to tend her.

"David," came her weak voice, broken by gasps, "This way." She held up a hand, indicating they must go down the hall to the right.

He stepped that way, not letting loose of her. If she were to pass out or fall, there would only be further injury.

And so, he pulled her down the corridor until he spotted the dining room. Surely, the kitchen was just beyond that. Directing her, he settled her into a chair.

"Let me—" she started.

He set a hand to her shoulder lest she try to rise. "Allow me."

As much as he didn't wish to leave her, he strode across the room to the doorway on the far side. Indeed, it did bring him into the kitchen. What did he need?

Cloths to make bandaging, perhaps a washbowl to clean them. He gathered what he could, deciding that a pot with water would work just as well as a fancy wash basin. He gripped the metal handle and gathered every cloth he could find in his other arm.

When he slipped back into the dining room, he was pleased to find Sadie where he'd left her. Setting the pot on the table nearby, he all but collapsed into the chair next to hers.

Grabbing for her right hand, he encountered only brief resistance.

He thrust one cloth into the water and used it to cleanse her cuts as he examined them. Some were small, others deeper and longer. How did this happen?

She sucked in a breath through her teeth, causing him to look up into her eyes.

That was perhaps a mistake. Her attention was on his ministrations, but her mouth was downturned. And the drawing together of her brows gave him the sense that more went on in her mind.

He refocused on his work and tried to push out calm words. "How did this happen?" His voice was shakier than he liked. But maybe she wouldn't notice.

"I...fell."

His attention was on her face then. But Sadie wouldn't look at him, keeping her gaze on the floor.

She fell? That much was obvious, but he would wager there was more to it. Something caused her to lose her balance.

He cleared his throat. Pressing a dry cloth to her now clean wounds, he then switched his attention to cleaning her left hand.

What *had* happened? Had the woman in the bed done something? Or Mrs. Wallem? The housekeeper had not seemed a violent person, but rather personable and timid even. It was the other woman, the one in the bed, that must have caused Sadie's fall. He was certain of it.

"Who was that?" Though as he said it, he feared he knew the answer. Hadn't Cook mentioned that Sadie's mother was not well? Still, he never dreamed her situation so dire.

That brought into question his involvement. For certain, this case became all the more difficult. As well as his understanding of the depth of Sadie's need grew.

He afforded her a glance.

She bit at her lip, as if she could keep the answer from coming out.

He halted his work and stared. The desire for her to answer overwhelmed him. She would have to get used to being honest about this. If not to him, then to whomever could help her.

Was that him? It couldn't be. He was set on departing in a few days. This was not what he needed; it was more than he could...he just couldn't get entangled in this.

At last, she let out a breath. "That was my mother."

He nodded, a slight movement, but didn't take his eyes off hers.

The green in Sadie's eyes became glassy. Were tears coming?

His heart seemed to leave his body all of a sudden. As if he could wrap her in his warmth, in his concern, and rescue her somehow.

Instead of leaning into him, she shivered.

He looked down at her hand and realized that he had started caressing her palm with his thumb. Even as he examined the skin, he noted that her hands appeared to be worked. More so than he would have expected of a fine, well-bred lady.

Though it did not put him off. He traced a finger over the hardening skin beneath her fingers. Would they become callouses in the coming days?

What was he doing? He couldn't fall more into this situation. It was imperative he lay out the truth for her and insist she find help in Wharton City or one of the surrounding towns. Someone who could fight for her.

At that thought, however, there was a tug deep within his chest. How could it be that *he* wanted to fight for her? That was utter nonsense. He couldn't. He shouldn't.

But as he set his gaze back on her, he knew that he would.

Sadie stirred. Her body ached. All over. And she was folded over in a strange position. Dare she open her eyes and find it all real—her mother's outburst, her own injuries, and perhaps the worst of it, David seeing it all?

But she could not deny the coming day any more than she could the morning she woke to discover her father gone. The day her life changed. Forever.

Lifting her eyelids, she saw her mother's bed. She sat up and everything ached. Yes, she had been seated by her mother's bed. It only made sense that she had lost her ability to maintain watch and fell over on the mattress. Indeed, as she searched her memory, she did catch an image of her leaning over to rest for a moment. How long ago was that?

She scanned the room. Where was Mother? Sadie was alone. Her body protested her movements—so sore. From her fall? Or from being bent over in the odd angle for who knew how long?

It mattered not, she needed to find Mother. What would happen if...if Mother wandered out of the house?

Please, God, don't let it be so.

She rose, biting back a moan as pain coursed through her. Reaching out a hand, she steadied herself with the back of the chair. And her hand stung.

Pulling it to herself, she looked at the chair for the culprit. It seemed innocent enough. Then she remembered—her bandages. Her hands had been cut and bruised.

With that came the memories of David tending her. His hands were gentle and warm. She had wanted to fall into him, take what comfort she could from his presence. But she hadn't. The horror of the situation and her worry of David's reaction had left her stymied. He seemed both put off and concerned. Yet he didn't shy away...didn't leave until she was bandaged and Mother had calmed.

Would that truly be the end though? Or would he insist on Mother being committed? Perhaps tell others of how bad the situation was.

Sadie had been strained beyond her limits to keep things stable. As stable as they could be. Her ability to pretend had worn thin. What now?

She moved out of Mother's room and down the hall, listening for any indication that Mother was nearby. Nothing. Then she prayed that Mother was still in the house. It was all for naught if she had gotten out and been discovered, or perhaps injured herself.

What would Sadie do in either scenario? She froze, her heart racing and panic claiming her mind. This would not help. Pressing down the anxious thoughts, she continued to wander the house.

It only took a glimpse into the parlor to begin to unravel what had happened. The room was utter chaos—books and furniture strewn about, upended. Even the curtains had been jerked askew until the rods barely held on.

And there, in the center of it all, lay Mother's form.

Sadie rushed to her side, through the maze of things on the floor and fighting her own pain. Kneeling, she placed a hand to Mother's back.

She breathed.

Thank You, Lord. Sadie let out the pent-up air.

Just then there was a creaking of the floorboards. Someone else was in the hall.

Sadie's pulse quickened. Who?

Of course...Mrs. Wallem must be up and about. Should she call to the woman? She wanted to alert Mrs. Wallem to her presence but didn't wish to rouse Mother.

Before she could decide, Mrs. Wallem walked by then halted and stepped a few paces back to look in.

"Miss Sadie!" she whispered. "What...?"

Sadie held up a hand and found reason to breathe again. She stood, with much effort, and crossed the room once more.

"I fell asleep in her room. She must have gotten up and come here looking for who knows what." Sadie dropped her head into her hand. The pain reminded her of her injury, and she pulled it back.

"Does it still hurt?" Mrs. Wallem's wide-eyed expression was kind and concerned. She reached for Sadie's right hand.

There was no point in lying. So Sadie nodded.

"Poor dear." Mrs. Wallem shook her head. "I'll be happy to have help. You are beyond exhausted."

Help! Sadie glanced at the sun streaming into the parlor. "Mrs. Wallem, what time is it?"

"It's near nine o'clock." Her brows furrowed.

"Nine o'clock?" Sadie gasped. She was supposed to be at the station to receive Aunt Jane at half past eight.

The woman nodded. "I was surprised you didn't rouse me so you could leave."

"Because I fell asleep," Sadie said as she rushed down the hall toward the door.

"Where are you going?" Mrs. Wallem called as her footfalls paced after Sadie.

"I have to go to the station...I have to find her!" How could she have let this happen? There was too much leaning on her for her to make such mistakes.

Mrs. Wallem grabbed her arm. "Not like that, you don't."

Sadie looked down. She was in her night shift. Nodding, she spun toward the stairs.

Again, Mrs. Wallem padded the floor right behind her.

They had Sadie dressed in a matter of moments. This had to stop. Perhaps soon it would. It was their only hope. Did she put too much on Aunt Jane's arrival? She'd best be mindful. The better to not be disappointed.

"I should change your bandages." Mrs. Wallem held Sadie's hands.

Sadie tugged them back and stepped into the hall. "There is no time for that."

"But..." Mrs. Wallem's voice was insistent.

"I...just can't. I'll manage until I get back." Sadie paused and turned. "With Aunt Jane."

And then she saw in Mrs. Wallem's eyes...a sense of dread. What brought that on? Did she simply worry that Aunt Jane would not be the salvation they needed? Or was it something else?

Sadie couldn't think like that. Not right now. She needed something to keep her moving forward.

As much as she could, she squeezed the older woman's hands before turning and slipping out the front door.

Hitching the wagon was more difficult than she'd wagered. And her hands were weary and burning by the time she pulled herself onto the bench. But it was done.

Sadie wiped a hand across her forehead. Would everything always be so difficult? She prayed not.

Jerking the reins, she urged the horse forward.

She resisted pushing the animal hard as they rushed toward Wharton City. She spotted the stagecoach near the telegraph office, but Aunt Jane was nowhere to be seen.

Sadie forced herself to stay calm as she brought the horse to a stop and stepped down. She took a couple of long strides before she realized she hadn't secured the animal. Spinning around a little too quickly, she gripped for the horse's harness to steady herself. She needed to slow down. And think.

After a moment, she felt more stable. She wrapped the reins to a nearby post and then slowed her steps as she moved toward the telegraph office.

Looking about the place, her heart fell. Aunt Jane wasn't here. Perhaps she had gone to the General Store? Or the café? Peering into the telegraph office, she spotted the customary line and frowned.

Moving back to the stagecoach, she caught sight of the driver.

"Sir," she called. But it wasn't until she neared that he looked at her.

"What can I do for you, miss?" The man appeared to be the rougher sort. Maybe that was needed in this sort of job. Either way, he did not seem untoward in his manner.

"Who...who did you have on the stagecoach today? Was there an older woman traveling with you?"

"Yes, there was."

Sadie's heart lightened.

"She and her daughter wandered off in that direction." He pointed toward the café.

But Sadie halted. "She and her daughter?" It couldn't be Aunt Jane then.

"Yes, miss. Them and a younger man were the only ones on the stage today." He watched her for a few minutes and then turned back to his work preparing the horses.

Sadie felt sick. She nodded her thanks to the man and moved around the stage. And she stepped to the boarded walkway where the many stares in her direction were as piercing and intense as ever.

She wanted to sink down to the edge of the walkway and settle into her dismay. But that wouldn't do. She best not give the people more to scorn than they already did.

So, she moved toward her cart and horse. But she could not resist taking a moment to calm herself with some gentle strokes on the mare's side and neck. Indeed, she leaned into the animal as if that would bring her comfort. It did not, but it kept her features from betraying her to the townsfolk.

Her eyes stung. What had happened to Aunt Jane? Had her children convinced her not to come? Alice and Martha had never been too fond of Sadie. They never could manage to just be civil with her. In fact, they had delighted in terrorizing their younger cousin on the few trips they had made to Wharton City. Yes, if they got wind of Aunt Jane's plans to come and help, they would certainly do everything they could to dissuade her. They must revel in Sadie's sad state that had become her way of life.

It was a shame.

But she couldn't much blame them. How could she expect anything different from them than the townsfolk?

"Miss?" a voice said from behind her.

Sadie sniffled and, pushing down her more difficult emotions, she turned.

A woman looked at her from the planked sidewalk. "Is something amiss?" The woman's voice was low, and she glanced about for some reason.

Sadie was surprised she—or anyone—would stop and speak to her amid all the stares and glares. But it couldn't be the entire town that had written her off. "I...was looking for someone to have arrived on the stage. Though it seems they did not come as expected."

The older woman pursed her lips. "I did see—"

"What are you doing out here, Maud?" a man stepped out of the General Store and aimed his question at the kind woman.

He glanced between Sadie and the woman. Was this her husband? His features shifted, a scowl now on his face. Stepping across the way, he took his wife's arm and tossing Sadie another look, said, "We need to get home."

The woman nodded and followed but offered Sadie an apologetic shrug.

Sadie was grateful for the woman's acknowledgement and attempt to help. She watched as the man ushered her back in the direction of the General Store.

Others moved in and out of the doorways lining the street. But as the couple moved farther off, they nearly plowed over two women who had stepped out of the mercantile. They excused themselves and continued on. Though Sadie then found herself staring at a somewhat surprised Aunt Jane. And beside her, stood Alice.

CHAPTER 9
Intentions

What had he done?

David looked across the fair-sized pond and reran the last day in his mind. It was disheartening to remember Sadie's injuries and her sadness. But he did relive it. As well as his decision to stay and do what he could for her.

Why had he done that?

It wasn't his responsibility. She wasn't his responsibility. Why hadn't he washed his hands of the whole situation and said farewell?

Because he cared.

And as much as he wanted to deny it, even rail against it, he couldn't help the twinge in his heart. When had he started to feel so for her?

Closing his eyes, he let out a long breath and pulled in another. The scent of the freshly blooming wildflowers graced him with their fragrance. It was calming.

How had he found himself out in the field, looking at these things? When had he left the porch and dirtied his fine shoes?

He couldn't say for certain. But he had felt drawn to this place. Something about it was peaceful, he had to admit. Is this what Brandon saw? Felt?

"Didn't expect to find you out here."

Was that Brandon? Had he conjured the man with his thoughts?

David kept his gaze on the horizon, refusing to turn and face his cousin.

"My mother said you won't be leaving tomorrow." Brandon's words were simple and unassuming.

David nodded. "That's true."

Brandon stepped up beside him near the water. "What changed your mind?"

The silence stretched between them.

"I guess I decided I was needed here." The words surprised even him.

"That you are." Something about Brandon's affirmation caught him off guard.

Did Brandon suspect that more went on between David and Sadie? That his feelings for her kept him here? For whatever reason, David didn't want Brandon to know how close to the truth he might be.

"The situation with her mother is...more difficult than I anticipated. I need to look into the legal precedents for this and have a serious talk with Sadie about her options." There. That seemed sound.

Brandon folded his arms across his chest. "Sure."

What did the man want from David? It didn't matter. That was all Brandon could pull from his cousin.

"What will you do about your cases back in Richmond? And your..." Brandon coughed before continuing, "your girl?"

Is that what Brandon thought? That David kept a lady back in Richmond and intended to play suitor to Sadie? Take advantage of the situation?

"I don't have a girl back in Richmond." Why had David felt the need to say that? It wasn't any of Brandon's business. David didn't owe him an explanation.

"Oh? That's not what I understood."

David felt Brandon's glare.

It probably would be best to clear the air. "I did."

"Hmmm..."

Was that all Brandon could offer? He had thought the worst of his cousin and that was his best response?

"Claire's affections..." David cleared his throat. "Transferred to another."

"Oh." The word was not a question.

Again, David wondered at his cousin's intrusiveness. "It is no matter."

Brandon shifted his weight. The silence again becoming thick between them.

What did David have to do? Why did he even care to ease this tension?

"So, there is no engagement. No plans. Nothing."

"I'm sorry to hear that," Brandon said simply.

When David glanced at Brandon, the man again watched the water rippling on the pond's surface, subject to the whim of the wind.

"Don't be." David's words were gentler than he'd have thought. He wanted to snap at Brandon for being so intrusive but found he couldn't. Something in him wanted to be more amiable. Was it his good breeding? "I'm not."

That was not the complete truth. Nor was it a total falsehood. True, David had been, and still was, burned by Claire's betrayal and rejection. And, yes, he had planned to marry her before discovering she had...a care for another.

"What," Brandon started, his words were measured, "What are your intentions with Sadie?"

Now David leveled his gaze on his cousin. "Intentions?"

Brandon did not seem the least bit fazed.

"I *intend* to offer her any legal advice I can and help her see her predicament for what it is."

Brandon widened his eyes. "And what is that exactly?"

David looked back to the horizon and sucked in a breath before pushing it out. "That, I'm afraid, I am not at liberty to discuss." Then he turned toward the homestead.

Brandon grabbed his arm as David made to pass. "I just want to be sure you won't make things worse for Sadie. She's been through a lot."

David shook off Brandon's easy grip. Then he walked up the hill without another word.

Sadie could hardly swallow against the reality of her predicament. Alice had come with Aunt Jane? Yet there she stood, sure as life, staring at Sadie.

"My goodness, Ma, if we didn't find Sadie Rose loafing about." Alice's tone bit at Sadie.

"Yes, I came to collect you...both."

"You came a bit late. Did you not know what time the stage came in?"

Sadie sighed. "I did. Things at home have been...a bit trying."

Alice looked her up and down. "No doubt. I can't fathom how your mother let you out of the house looking like that."

Indeed, Sadie knew it was true. She was certainly disheveled and harried despite Mrs. Wallem's best efforts. What could the woman accomplish with such horrid materials?

Sadie looked at her aunt, curious as to what the woman thought. Her kind eyes looked Sadie up and down. She must have seen what Alice —and everyone else—saw. And Sadie wished she wasn't so bothered by the realization. But she was.

She avoided Alice's gaze, which could be felt just as well without looking. The woman glared at her. Judgment oozing from her being.

How would Sadie survive the coming days or even weeks? Still, it had to be better than the existence she and Mrs. Wallem had been living. Didn't it?

"Well?" Alice's sharp retort cut through the air. "Are we to stand out here in the open all day? Or do you intend to take us to your mother? That *is* why we came, isn't it?"

Sadie nodded, every bit of her ire sucked out of her. "I...do need to stop by and see Dr. Norwood."

Alice rolled her eyes. "Very well, then. Go. I will not abide my mother being subjected to this level of floating dirt." She made a face. "So, I beseech you to be on your way and be quick about it."

Nodding once, Sadie moved off toward the clinic. She held her head down the whole of the short stroll, only glancing up to knock.

Dr. Norwood was at the door in a few moments. His eyes widened slightly when he saw it was Sadie. "What is the matter, Miss Perkins?"

Wasn't it only a couple of days since she was right here begging the doctor for more medicine? And here she was again. "We are in need of some—"

"You need more medicine?" The lilt of the doctor's tone betrayed his surprise.

Sadie swallowed and found herself unable to meet his gaze. "Mother...that is, the bottle was spilled."

"Is that what happened to your hands?"

She looked at him. His eyes were on her bandaged palms.

What could she say? There was nothing she could add, so she nodded.

"Perhaps I should examine them." He reached for her right hand.

She jerked them to herself. "I am quite well. Nothing requiring attention, I assure you."

He gave her a hard look and paused, as if weighing his options. "All right, Miss Perkins. But I only have one more bottle to spare right now. I have sent for more, but it will take time."

She peered up at him. "I am sorry I have to ask for it."

"I know." His words softened. "Perhaps we need to have another conversation about this."

The warmth drained from her features. Would he press the issue now?

"When you have a moment." His gaze moved down the boardwalk to where her cart awaited. "I see you have company."

Sadie shifted her focus and spotted that Alice had managed to get herself and Aunt Jane into the cart. Letting out a breath, Sadie couldn't help but be thankful they would be underway sooner rather than later.

Dr. Norwood sighed. "Maybe your relations can talk some sense to you about your mother's situation. She needs more than you can provide." Then he slipped within the clinic.

How much more of this could Sadie take? If it kept her mother safe and cared for, she could endure. But the doctor's words were like a punch to her gut. Was she attempting the impossible? Aunt Jane had her own life. She couldn't stay forever. And when she left, Sadie and Mrs. Wallem would be right back where they started. Could she endure that? How could she not try?

Dr. Norwood reappeared with the medicine bottle in hand. "Please be sparing." He let out a breath.

Was he, too, put out with her now? Just one more person she had disappointed.

"Thank you, doctor. I will." Then she nodded and turned. But she kept her eyes to the boards under her feet. How could she look at him again? How could she hold her head up in this town? Would she ever be able to do so again?

As she neared the cart, Alice's words added more weight to her already downcast spirit. "Thank the Lord. I didn't know how much more of this place we could tolerate. For certain, there is a now a layer of dirt on both of us."

Sadie bit her lip and nodded but couldn't look up. She tucked the medicine in her reticule and hauled herself onto the driver's bench. It was no easy task with the tender flesh on her hands burning as she did so.

But she managed to keep her whimpers at bay. She was determined not to betray her additional weakness to her knife-tongued cousin.

The tightness in her chest eased only a little as she directed the horse and cart away from town and prayed her cousin would keep quiet. There was little more Sadie's spirit could bear right now.

Blessedly, the remainder of the trip to the house was spent in silence. There was, however, the occasional huff and gasp from Alice, but no other biting comments. And though the trip was longer than she ever remembered it being, they arrived intact.

Sadie climbed down and came around the wagon to help her aunt dismount.

Alice shoved her way out first, sliding between Sadie and the cart. "I don't want Mother to slip. And you appear," she directed her gaze to Sadie's wrapped hands, "Less capable."

Sadie took a step back, nodding as she did so. How was she to endure such treatment? As if her situation wasn't difficult enough?

Perhaps this had been a mistake. Then again, she knew Aunt Jane's presence was much needed.

After Aunt Jane was safely on the ground, Sadie said, "I will tend to the horse momentarily. Let me get you two inside."

Alice frowned. "You will tend to the horse and cart?"

Sadie nodded.

An exasperated sound came from Alice, but there was nothing Sadie could do. She couldn't conjure up help where there was none.

Sadie grabbed for Aunt Jane's suitcase and stepped toward the front door.

"Are we to carry our own things in?" Alice's surprised words shot into Sadie.

She sighed and squared her shoulders. There was little reason to continue to avoid the issue. "Since my...father has left...we don't have the assistance we once did."

"I see," Alice said as she looked at her mother. "This is unacceptable."

"That is the way of it. I...wish it could be otherwise." She bit her lower lip, hating that her sentiment slipped out.

A thick silence fell over the three women for several moments. And Sadie braced herself for whatever was to come from Alice's mouth.

"Well then, that...is that," Aunt Jane chimed in. Her words were gentle and yet still firm. A message to Alice? Then Aunt Jane regarded the house. "Shall we get settled?"

Sadie nodded. "This way, please." She led Aunt Jane and Alice into the house.

Where was Mrs. Wallem? Sadie had anticipated the woman would be ready to receive them. But she was nowhere to be seen.

"Mrs. Wallem?" she called, her face warming at what Alice must be thinking.

Nothing.

Sadie set the suitcase down. "If you'll give me just a moment."

"Whatever for?" Alice's voice had already started grating on Sadie's nerves.

But she didn't even attempt a response as she moved away from the pair.

Sadie passed the parlor, which had been set aright. She owed Mrs. Wallem a debt for that. Then Sadie moved toward Mother's room. The door was closed. What might await her on the other side?

She knocked lightly. "Mrs. Wallem?" she spoke softly, praying that her aunt and cousin wouldn't hear the desperation in her voice.

The door cracked open. Mrs. Wallem's darkened eyes met Sadie's. "Miss Sadie!" There was no denying the relief in her voice.

"Who is there?" Mother's voice sounded angry.

Sadie met Mrs. Wallem's gaze again.

The woman shook her head.

Sadie slipped a hand into her reticule, pulling out the laudanum.

Mrs. Wallem let out a tight breath at the sight.

Indeed, they would have to talk. It would not do to be constantly drugging Mother.

"Sadie Rose? Is that you?" Mother's voice had an edge to it.

"Yes, Ma. I'm here." Sadie glanced around Mrs. Wallem.

Mother glared at her. "Where have you been?"

Sadie stepped within. "I brought Aunt Jane and Alice here. They want to see you." But dare she expose her relations to Mother yet? They were bound to find out, though. Maybe there would be some easing of Alice's ire once she saw exactly what Sadie had been dealing with.

"Jane is here?" Mother's voice told of her interest.

Sadie released a pent up breath. "Yes. And she is eager to see you."

Mrs. Wallem's eyes widened.

Sadie set a hand to her arm as she passed into the room. "It will be all right," she whispered.

"What are you saying?" Mother's voice rose again.

"I was asking Mrs. Wallem to bring some tea to the parlor."

Mother's accusing stare settled on Sadie. Oh, what did it matter?

Sadie took her mother's arm. "Shall we tend to our guests?"

But Mother just stared. Then patted Sadie's hand. "You're a good girl."

Sadie was tempted to let the rare praise settle into her being, but there was not time. She urged her mother forward and down the hall. With each step, she both dreaded and eased at the thought of the coming interaction.

But as they turned the corner and saw that Aunt Jane and Alice remained at the entrance, Sadie had a thought that all might be well.

She smiled at her aunt as they neared. "See, Mother, Aunt Jane has come to see you."

"Jane?" Mother looked over the woman. Then turned to Sadie. "Where is Jane?"

CHAPTER 10
Disheartened

D avid rushed into the homestead and let the front door shut hard behind him. He didn't care. How could Brandon be so...so bold? His cousin didn't understand. He couldn't. Yes, Brandon had no idea what he was talking about. David was not interested in Sadie in that way. She was a client. A job. That was all. Yes, he felt bad for her situation, but that was pity. Not tender feelings.

Storming through the great room and into the hall, David stomped into his borrowed room. His whole being seemed tight, as if his muscles were coiled and ready to strike. Not that he had ever done so. Only a lesser man would work out one's anger on another person.

But he couldn't help but wonder if slamming his fists into the wall would help. Even a little.

He stared at the wall but instead stepped to the wash basin and splashed water on his face.

For certain, he was hopeless.

No, what Brandon said wasn't true. So why let it bother him?

Glancing around the room did nothing to assuage David's ire. The space was so confining all of a sudden. He longed for his own bed chambers—expansive by comparison and filled with his things. Samuel's room was oddly bare. David wondered at the boy's life. Was he truly so simple? Or did the things he valued not go into a bedroom?

Still, David was thankful for the youngster and for the afforded privacy. How much worse it would be if he had nowhere to go and be away from all of it.

David wiped his face with the provided towel.

Brandon's questions came back to him. Did the man think so little of his cousin? That he would play act with a lady when he was otherwise engaged? David frowned. Nothing could be further from the truth. Claire was...no longer his concern. But the sting of her rejection still soured his stomach.

He fought the urge to douse his face again. Would that sober his mind?

Where had he gone wrong? Perhaps he had not been the most attentive beau. But he worked toward a partnership in the firm. Maybe he had not been overly affectionate. Yet did that truly earn the resulting scorn?

Though it nagged at him. Had he really cared for Claire? Or was his pride simply wounded by her actions? Those were hard questions. And he didn't want to face the answers.

"Sorry, Mr. Anderson!" the voice came from the doorway.

David turned to find Samuel just inside the room.

"I didn't mean to intrude." The lad turned. "I can come back later."

Shaking his head, David thrust the towel onto the stand and stepped toward the youngster. "Do not worry yourself. Please," he said, waving a hand, "it *is* your room after all."

Samuel offered a smile. "Thanks. I just need to grab another set of trousers. Ma said these have to be washed."

David lowered his gaze to the boy's pants. Indeed, they were filthy. What had he been doing? But David refrained from asking. It wasn't as if he didn't know. Sleeping in the hay loft, mucking stalls, and all manner of work about this dirty ranch. No wonder his trousers were in such a state.

Samuel moved into the room and to his trunk. He pulled out the clothing he sought and nodding to David, crossed toward the door once more. Then paused as if remembering something.

"Oh, and Ma wanted me to find you."

"Whatever for?"

"It's about lunch time. And you know how Cook can be..."

Yes, he did. The woman became rather intolerable when one arrived late to her table. Her glare alone could scorch a man.

David nodded as he breathed in the scent of potatoes and beef. "I'll be there soon."

Samuel dipped his head and then left the room.

And David gave himself a once over in the mirror. How had he gotten so caught up in this? He needed to have a chat with Sadie. Someone had to be frank with her about her mother's condition. If she could be convinced to commit her mother, then that made his job easier. And his involvement less deep.

He would ask if anyone was headed in that direction—or could be —this afternoon.

With his mind made up, he straightened his shirt and set out toward the dining room. No need to upset Cook.

Sadie fought down the apprehension rising in her as she watched Aunt Jane and Alice's reaction.

Aunt Jane pursed her lips and arched her brows. It was not promising.

"Mother, you know this is Aunt Jane," Sadie said, trying to disguise the waver in her voice.

Her mother studied Aunt Jane, as if trying to work out who she was. "I am very pleased to meet you."

"Good Lord in heaven, she's gone mad," Alice announced.

Aunt Jane gave her a sharp look but didn't contradict her.

"She has had...a lot of trouble, since Father..." Sadie couldn't finish her statement. She just couldn't make herself say the words.

Alice's green eyes fairly glowed as she glared at Sadie. "She's a lunatic."

"Now, Alice," Aunt Jane started, "Let's not—"

"Tell me I'm wrong." Alice's gaze shifted between the women there. "Go ahead."

Even as Sadie's face burned, she couldn't find any words in that moment.

"I *welcome* anyone telling me otherwise." Alice might as well have spit on them for the disgust in her voice. Then she leveled her gaze on Sadie again. "And just what do you expect us to do?"

"I...just needed someone...the thing is, Mrs. Wallem and I have..." Why was her voice so timid all of a sudden? How could she let Alice bully her? Bully Mother?

"What?" Alice's retort was sharp. Then she stepped closer to her mother. "She doesn't need assistance. She needs a madhouse!" Alice tugged at her mother. "Come, we need to get on the next stage out of here."

Then the stirring in Sadie's stomach swelled. And she burst forth. "No!"

Alice turned, her eyes wide. "No?"

"No." Sadie handed her mother off to Mrs. Wallem. "Please, see Mother to the parlor. We shall be along shortly."

And she watched as Mrs. Wallem obeyed. Once Mother was around the corner, Sadie turned back to her relations and firmed her tone. "I will *not* have my mother in an asylum."

Alice rolled her eyes. "That is where she belongs."

Sadie stepped closer to the woman she had pleaded with to come. The woman who was her last hope. "Aunt Jane, you must understand. Those places...the asylums...they do things. The kinds of things you wouldn't wish on the vilest person."

"Don't talk to her about that. You're only making this worse." Alice tried to slide between her mother and Sadie.

But Sadie caught the older woman's free hand. "Please, hear me out. They...use electricity on them. To shock them. And they..." Sadie's voice caught as the thought of her mother enduring these things nearly brought her to tears. "They perform lobotomies."

Alice stilled, but her jaw tightened. "She's just trying to play on your sympathies. There's no reason we should—"

Aunt Jane gripped her daughter's arm. And her eyes had softened. "We will not abandon our dear ones when they are in such need."

Sadie swallowed hard and avoided her cousin's eyes. "It is my prayer and my hope that Mother's severely addled mind is only because of Father's leaving. It is possible she will improve with time and rest."

"Is that what the physician said?" Alice's words shoved into the middle of the conversation.

"No," Sadie admitted. "But I cannot give up hope." In that moment, she looked at Alice, beseeching her silently to understand, to have compassion.

Aunt Jane latched a hand onto Sadie's. "What do you need of us, Sadie Rose?"

Relief rushed through Sadie. There *was* hope!

"You can't be serious." Alice pulled back from her mother, eyeing the woman.

"If there is a chance she can be recovered. We will embrace it."

Alice shook her head. "I will have no part of this." She whirled toward the front door.

"Do as you must," Aunt Jane called after her, "But I am staying. That is final."

That halted Alice mid-step. She spun back toward her mother and glared once more at Sadie. "If you must, I will stay and assist as well. But know this, come one week from today, I will be the first in line to have her committed. And I won't be swayed by the tears of a spoiled princess."

She moved past Sadie and Aunt Jane, bumping Sadie as she did so.

"Where are you going?" Aunt Jane called.

"To the guest rooms," she said as she mounted the stairs.

Aunt Jane offered Sadie a sympathetic, small smile. "Please, take me to your mother. I want to see if we can clear up a few things for her."

Sadie smiled back, and her gratitude was so great, she was certain it was palpable to her aunt. "This way."

As they made their way to the parlor to join Mother and Mrs. Wallem, Sadie tossed a glance in the direction of Alice's retreating figure. If Sadie was to keep Mother safe and comfortable at home, she had her work cut out for her. Convincing a jaded Alice could very well prove more difficult than pulling Mother back from the abyss.

CHAPTER 11

Difficulties

To say that the ride to the Perkins' home had been uncomfortable would be an understatement. David did his best to not enlist Brandon for anything conversation related or otherwise. He was still a bit sore at his cousin for the intrusive nature of their last interaction.

Still, he was relieved to be traveling with Brandon...better than that buffoon Junior. David had learned to take the pluses as they came. So, a trip into Wharton City with Brandon it was.

Though, the night between his desire of this jaunt and the actual visit had seemed long. David was tempted to yawn at the very thought of the hours he had lain in bed, thinking about what he would say to Sadie, how he would address the issue...all of it. But he was no closer to hammering out a plan for his entreaty than he had been when he'd requested this trip yesterday afternoon.

No amount of sleep, no amount of preparation would do.

"We're here." Brandon's baritone cut through his thoughts.

He glanced around and, indeed, they had pulled up to the Perkins' home. Dipping his head once, David moved to drop down onto the roadway in front of the house.

"I'll be back in a couple of hours," Brandon said as David's feet landed solidly on the earth.

David nodded and grabbed his case. "Thanks."

Coming around the cart and horse, David straightened his jacket. A client. That's all this was...a meeting with a client.

He paused as he came to the door. Closing his eyes, he sucked in a breath and knocked.

The horse snorted behind him. How long would Brandon linger? Did he only wish to ensure David was welcomed in? Or did he stay to assure himself there was proper chaperonage?

Creaking, the door eased open. Someone needed to tend to that.

But he focused as the person beyond the door was revealed. Mrs. Wallem greeted him with a smile. "Mr. Anderson, what can I do for you?"

"Good day, Mrs. Wallem." He gave a slight nod. "I'm here to speak with Miss Perkins."

Mrs. Wallem rubbed her hands on her apron. "Right this way." She turned and ushered him within. "And Mr. Miller? Will he be joining you?"

David shook his head. "He has other things to attend to."

"Very well." Then she led him into the house.

He spotted the dining room as they passed it on their way, he supposed, to the parlor. His mind flitted back to he and Sadie sitting at the table, her hands in his. She had trusted him in that moment. Completely. Trusted in his concern for her and his ability to take care of her. The thought drove a pang into his chest.

Was he doing the right thing for *her*? Or for himself?

Perhaps, he told himself, they are one and the same. She needed someone to tell her the truth. And he needed to not be involved any deeper than necessary. This was right.

The smell of vegetables and chicken wafted through the air. It occurred to him that he had not noticed the scent of food the other times he had been here. Because it wasn't mealtime? Or because caring for Sadie's mother had taken too much of their time and effort to have anything to spare for such niceties?

He hadn't more time to dwell on that before Mrs. Wallem slowed near the parlor. Opening the door, she announced to those within. "Mr. Anderson is here to see you, Miss Sadie."

"Oh, show him in," she called. Her voice was stronger, brighter even. But there was another voice within. Who sat with her?

He stepped into the parlor and spotted an older woman sitting across from her. Was this her aunt? The one who had come to assist?

Sadie stood and stepped to him. "Mr. Anderson, I was not expecting you today. Did we have an appointment?"

He shook his head. "I just wanted—" He paused and cleared his throat. "Needed to have a discussion with you."

"Very well then. I would like you to meet my aunt, Jane Higgins. Aunt Jane, this is my lawyer, Mr. David Anderson."

The elder lady rose. "How good of you, Mr. Anderson, to take care of my cousin's daughter."

Her what? Hadn't Sadie just called the woman her aunt?

"Oh, I am sorry. Have I caused some sort of confusion?"

David looked between the two women. "You and Mrs. Perkins... sisters? Or cousins?"

"I understand now. Eugenia is my cousin. But she wasn't blessed with siblings...or cursed, whatever may be your pleasure on the matter. We have always been more as sisters. So, when Sadie was born, she insisted I be Aunt Jane to her daughter."

Ah. That cleared things a bit.

"Which, I must be checking in on Eugenia," Mrs. Higgins said. "Please, excuse me while I do so."

"Of course." David stepped to the side to let her pass.

Then he and Sadie were alone. He let his gaze wander over her. Her hands were bandaged still, but she actually looked more well. Perhaps with her mother's cousin in the house, she had been more rested. She wore it well.

"Please, come in. Have a seat." Sadie moved back to the settee she had been at previously. "Did you need to speak with me about something? Or is this a social call?" Something in her eyes seemed to sparkle at that comment. Was she so bold? Or was that a tease?

Either way, he stepped forward and settled into a chair nearby. "I have something to discuss."

"All right." She ran a hand along her pressed skirt and then clasped her hands in her lap. Indeed, her eyes were brighter and her affect much improved. After one night's rest? Or was there more to it? Dare he hope some of that lightness was because of his arrival?

He chided himself. That was exactly the kind of nonsense thinking that he needed to avoid.

"Before we wander into other matters, I think I need to apologize." Sadie offered him a sweet smile.

It melted his core. Why would she need to ask his pardon? Whatever for? Unsure of himself, he remained silent.

"The last time you were here, I was...rather apprehensive. I don't think I thanked you properly for how you helped me."

"It was nothing." He rubbed hands over his knees.

"It was more than that to me." Her words were so earnest it caused his breath to catch. "Not only did you care for me so well, you...didn't scorn me because of my mother's behavior."

He looked down at his hands. How was he to proceed?

"So, Mr. Anderson...David, I want you to know how much your kindness meant to me." Her features softened and her cheeks colored the slightest bit. As if she were warmed by his presence. Or did she warm at the memories of their closeness the same as he?

This only made his purpose here more difficult. But he could not let it. There was a need for honesty. And he would have it guide him and his words.

"Miss Perkins, I—"

"Sadie," she insisted.

He paused, but briefly. "Sadie...I need to speak with you regarding your mother."

Her smile fell and an uneasiness settled over her features. Though she did nothing to dissuade his words. Well, nothing more than look at him as if she admired him. Truly admired him.

He looked toward the window. "Your mother is not—ah—faring as well as I had thought."

She pulled in a shaky breath.

But he forced himself to continue. "And when someone...such as your mother, is not...as she could be, it makes things...difficult."

He glanced at Sadie. Her features were contorted. As if he were as confusing as he sounded to himself.

"What I mean to say is that your mother is not as I expected."

"Yes, that is true." The apprehension had soaked into her voice. It seemed some of her timidity returned.

"I just..." Was he sweating? Goodness, this was not going well.

"Please," she said, intruding on his thoughts, "You can just say it. I trust you."

He met her gaze again. How was it possible to feel so drawn in by someone when there was such physical distance between their bodies?

"Sadie, are you going mad, or am I?" A feminine voice called from the direction of the stairs. "Have you resorted to talking to the walls?"

A figure came to the door—a woman who appeared a younger version of Mrs. Higgins.

"Pardon me, sir. I did not know we had company." The woman looked from him to Sadie and back.

Sadie looked away as if uneasy.

"Not necessary," David said as he stood. "I'm representing Miss Perkins and her mother."

"A lawyer?" The woman's eyebrow piqued. "How interesting!"

Goodness, the woman poured it on thick.

"I'm Alice Higgins, Sadie's cousin." She stepped closer.

"Ah. It is a pleasure to meet you." He held his ground.

"I assure you, the pleasure is mine. I can't tell you how relieved I am that dear Sadie has such good help with this horrible mess."

"Ah, yes. Well—"

"Miss Sadie!" It sounded as if Mrs. Wallem ran toward the parlor. She certainly sounded frightened.

Sadie came to life, rushing to the doorway and looking down the hall. "What is it?"

David drew up behind her. He surprised himself when the urge to curl her into himself came over him. As if he could protect her from anything and everything. Nonsense.

"Miss Sadie," an out of breath Mrs. Wallem gasped as she came to a halt by Sadie. "Sheriff McAllen and two other men are outside. Nailing a notice to the house."

"A what?" Sadie gathered her voluminous skirt and, without a thought for herself, took off toward the front door.

"Sadie," David called as he followed. "Sadie, wait. You can't just go barging up to..." David came to a halt behind her as she flung the door open.

Indeed, there was the sheriff and two other men just outside.

"What is the meaning of this?" Sadie demanded.

The ire of her voice surprised David.

He stepped in front of her. "Sheriff, what is this about?" David craned his neck to get a look at the notice.

"Who are you? Are you that Miller relation come to town?" the man said. He did not sound pleased about it.

"That is not important. I'm David Anderson, legal counsel for the Perkins family."

"Ah," one of the other men said as he stepped to David. "Then you'll be here to make sure this happens all legal like."

David narrowed his gaze on the man. He did not like the stranger already.

"Sheriff," the man said, though he didn't shift his glare any farther from David than to look him up and down. Sizing him up?

"The bank is taking possession of this house, Miss Perkins." Sheriff McAllen smirked. "As payment for the debt your family owes the good people of this town. You have exactly one hour to get your things and leave."

Sadie shouldered past David. "You can't be serious."

"I assure you, I am." Sheriff McAllen seemed to be fighting a smile. Was it more than his job behind this? Did he take some sick pleasure in evicting her and her mother?

"Now, let's not be rash." David's hand touched her arm. "Sheriff, there must be more leniency you can offer. An hour is absurd."

Sadie couldn't process what was happening. An hour? How could this be? As if she and Mother hadn't had a difficult enough time. Now they would be pressed until crushed?

It couldn't be. Surely God would not allow such. Yet here Sheriff McAllen and his deputy stood. Ready to enforce the edict.

"Who might you be, sir?" David again took the initiative, looking to the man in the suit.

The stranger opened his mouth, but Sheriff McAllen cut him off. "This is our new banker. Straight from Chicago."

"I apologize, I did not catch your name." David's focus was on the man, all but ignoring the intrusive sheriff.

But Sheriff McAllen insisted on intervening. "I didn't throw it."

Tension building between the two men beside her was thick.

Sadie spoke up. "Sheriff, you can't just show up and expect us to pack like this. We need time. And—"

"I can. And I am." Sheriff McAllen leaned back on his heels, crossing his arms over his chest. "It's my sworn duty to make sure the citizens of Wharton City abide by the law. *Every* citizen."

Something powerful rose in Sadie. Was it protectiveness toward her mother, or had she reached the end of her ability to endure the undue harassment of the townsfolk? She didn't know. But the burning in the pit of her stomach grew.

She stomped to the notice and ripped it off its nail.

"Miss Perkins!" Sheriff McAllen stepped toward her.

David again inserted himself. Not that she needed him to fight her battles. But he was on her side. And she sorely needed an ally right now.

"You will hand that over at once." The sheriff's glare hardened as he stuck out a hand. Did he expect her to plea for her home? To hand over the paper and apologize? He would be waiting a long time if that was the case.

She pressed it to her chest.

David put out a hand as well. "May I see it?"

Should she trust him? Would he hand it back to the sheriff? Or would he back her up as her proxy? Did she want him to?

His gaze was soft and his entreaty, while firm, didn't have the same biting edge the sheriff's words had.

She handed it over. Why did it make her feel so defeated?

David ignored the sheriff's exasperated press of breath and read the notice.

Sadie didn't know what to do with her hands. Or herself, for that matter.

"Mr. Anderson, I assure you everything is above board." The still unknown man said. "We have every right to confiscate Mr. Perkins' assets to repay his debts."

"It seems you are indeed in error." David glanced up. "Mister?"

"Collins," the man offered.

"Mr. Collins," David started as he waved the notice. "Perhaps you are unaware of a few things. Since 1848, a woman's property owned separately from the marital assets, cannot be held liable for her husband's debts."

Could that be true? Hope sparked anew in Sadie's chest. Dare she rely on it?

Mr. Collins' lips became a thin line. "But I don't understand. Isn't the home part of the joint property?"

"As a fact, it is not." David's gaze moved between Sheriff McAllen and Mr. Collins. "The house is a portion of the property Mrs. Perkins inherited prior to the marriage."

Mr. Collins' brow furrowed. "Are you quite certain? I was sure my lawyers looked into the legalities of—"

"I don't know what to tell you," David pressed out as he jerked the paper once more. "That is the law. And these are the facts."

Sadie chanced a glance at Sheriff McAllen. The man's face reddened. If he stewed any hotter, steam would come out his ears.

"So, as you can see," David said matter-of-factly as he turned to the sheriff. "Your notice is entirely premature at best, an overreach at worst. And I intend to find out which."

The strength behind David's words touched Sadie's core. She hadn't felt so...safe. So...cared for in quite some time.

But the men facing her and David did not seem pleased. Of course, they wouldn't be. David had outwitted them. What would she have done without his knowledge and skill? He had kept a level head and argued the facts. She was all fire and passion in the moment. Two things that would certainly have come to naught.

The sheriff and the banker exchanged a look.

Mr. Collins shrugged. "I will concede the point..."

Sadie's heart soared.

"For *now*."

David's expression held, unchanging. He did not seem the least bit intimidated.

"But I assure you," Mr. Collins said, "I will have my people research this."

With that, the man turned and walked away.

Sheriff McAllen uncrossed his arms and grunted. "This isn't over."

The relief pouring through Sadie was short-lived at the sheriff's assertion. Could David continue to defend her and Mother against this action? Would his argument hold up? She wished she knew.

The sheriff put a hand out again. "I'll be taking that."

David jerked it farther away from the man's hand. "I think I'll hold onto it."

"Suit yourself." Sheriff McAllen whirled around and signaled the deputy to follow. "We have more...important things to attend to."

Sadie refused to give way to the sting of his words. Yes, she knew the townsfolk did not believe her worth much. But they weren't right. They couldn't be.

She shifted her focus to David. His features were set, and rather uninvitingly so, as he watched the three leave.

Once the dust kicked up by the horse's hooves covered any more hint of the departure of the three interlopers, David looked to her.

She set a hand to his arm. "Thank you."

His gaze settled on hers for a long moment. "That is not necessary. It was my job." The words were gentle. As if he somehow said them to himself.

"Still...I don't know what I would have done had you not been here."

He laid a hand over hers. "Then it is a good thing I was here." A smile played at the corners of his mouth. And the warmth of his touch shot heat across her skin all the way to her heart. What was this thing between them? Was it just as he insisted—his job and nothing else? For her part, there was no denying the tug on her heart when he was near.

"Sadie, I—"

"Whatever is going on out here?" Alice's higher pitched voice cut through the moment. "And what is with all the haste?"

Stepping outside, Alice looked from David to Sadie and back.

David released Sadie's hand and dropped his arm, causing hers to slide back to her side. Did he not wish to be thought associated with her beyond the lawyer-client relationship?

He looked at Alice. "It is nothing to concern yourself with, Miss Higgins."

"I should hope not," came her retort. "Sadie sure can get herself into trouble."

"Oh?" He looked to Sadie, brow piqued.

"If you want to hear the tales of Sadie's bad choices," Alice said as she looped an arm around David's and drew him in the direction of the house, "you may have to stay for lunch."

As they slipped back within, Sadie took in a long breath. Perhaps it was best Alice interrupted them. There was too much to think through. Too much to sort out in her own mind. If ever she could.

Pushing the pent-up air out of her lungs, she gripped her skirt and stepped into the house.

CHAPTER 12
Determined

avid pushed his plate away. The meal had been more than satisfying. In truth, the food reminded him of the fare he was used to. Where had Mrs. Wallem learned to bake? Somewhere farther East? She certainly didn't have the same culinary repertoire as Cook.

"And so, she walked away. Without so much as an apology. Can you imagine?" Alice finished the umpteenth story of the hour.

True, he had found himself smiling, even at times laughing, at Sadie's stories. So often she was driven by emotion. And her choices, at times, belied her station. Still, he couldn't help but steal glimpses of her, cheeks reddened. How was it that she became all the more pleasing to look at? And then he would avert his gaze. As he did now.

"I thank you," he said, grinning at the women around the table. "For the meal and for the fine conversation."

"If you call it that," Alice interjected. "We must have spent the whole time talking about Sadie."

David kept a straight face. How could he communicate that he hadn't minded that one bit?

"No one forced you to tell those stories." Sadie looked at her plate. Was she avoiding Alice's gaze? Or his?

This had been a fine time—a moment to sit back and enjoy. Not have to go and be and do. Yes, the Miller Ranch was slow paced enough, but he didn't feel so relaxed there. Not like here. With Sadie.

Where had that thought come from? It was dangerous.

He pulled himself back to the moment to find Alice glaring at Sadie. Then turning away as if she cared not what her cousin thought. Not that anyone would believe that. No one would spend an hour telling all manner of embarrassing stories about someone who didn't bother them in the least. Were they told for the purpose of putting Sadie off? Or for his benefit? To ensure his good opinion of Sadie was tarnished?

Nothing could be further from the truth. If anything, he felt closer to her...even found her more endearing. And that had to stop. Now.

He cleared his throat. All eyes turned on him.

Goodness...was that necessary?

"That was delicious." He let his smile linger.

Mrs. Wallem nodded as she stood and gathered an armload of dishes.

The flavor of the herbed potatoes tempted him to indulge further, though he thought better of it. "And I appreciate the fine company."

Alice's eyes lit up. Was she so eager for his attention? That didn't bode well.

He rose, setting his gaze on Sadie. "But I must excuse myself to speak with Miss Perkins."

Sadie looked at him. It caught him for a moment, and he forgot what he was doing.

"Mr. Anderson?" Alice leaned toward him.

"Yes?" He forced himself to turn in her direction.

"Are you unwell?" The insufferable woman pried too much.

"Yes, Miss Higgins. I was just...deep in thought."

When he glanced in Sadie's direction, she attempted to hide a smile as she stood. Soon after she gained her feet, she faced him. "Shall we retire to the parlor?"

He nodded and reminded himself that he must keep his wits about him. There was no room for error here. He must set her straight as to his purpose here and find a way to speak with her about her mother's condition, as he had planned to do before they were interrupted earlier.

Sadie led the way out of the dining room, into the hall, and to the parlor.

He maintained a good two feet of distance behind her. While walking, he considered his forthcoming words, growing even more determined to say what needed to be said. After all, he had never been one to be swayed by a pretty face. And he wouldn't be now.

She did not slow her pace as she moved into the parlor and to that same settee she had vacated earlier that day. Was she so confident? Would she still be after he said his piece?

His steps within were slower. And he paused by the door. It should remain open for propriety's sake, yet he wasn't certain he wished for her cousin or Aunt Jane to overhear. For certain, their conversation need not reach her mother's ears...if the woman could make sense of such things anymore.

When he looked in her direction again, he found that she watched him. Studied him, actually.

"Mr. Anderson...David, I am glad you were here to stop those men from..." Her words caught in her throat and it seemed for a moment as if she would not continue. But she did, "throwing my mother and I out of our home."

He nodded, unable to naysay her and unwilling to garner more admiration from her.

Sadie met his gaze again. "I will confess, I was..." A sound somewhat between a chuckle and a choke came out. "...at first, that is...I was bothered by your intrusion."

That surprised him.

"It's not as if I can't take care of myself."

Could she? The situation had seemed quite desperate before he stepped in. He opened his mouth to speak into the pause, but she continued before he could.

"Still, I am able to admit when my...emotion gets the better of me. I did need you. And I am grateful to you for stepping in even though I didn't realize I needed you to."

The approval shining in her eyes was almost more than he could bear. Certainly in light of what he had to say.

He swallowed as he moved closer to where she sat. "I am likewise glad I was able to help."

She beamed.

He played with the cuff of his right sleeve. "That is, to do my job."

Her smile wavered.

He looked toward the window at the brightness of the afternoon sun on the back of the house. Anywhere but at her.

"Sadie..." Her name fell from his lips with emotion he did not disguise. Could he not try harder? "Miss Perkins, I want to be as up front as I can."

Her gaze narrowed slightly. And her mouth had a downturned slant to it.

He would have to be at peace with her disapproval if he was to distance himself. Though it was against his better judgment, he took a seat beside her. The lines on her features were even more evident up close.

"There are...obstacles in this case. Some that we can work through more easily than others, I'm afraid."

One of her eyebrows arched.

He needed to be clearer, to come right out with it. "But I think... that is, I believe...our chances are good."

The muscles of her face relaxed. And relief washed over her features. Even bringing a slight slump to her shoulders. Did she think that was all? He needed to push forward. Who knew when their time would be cut short by an interloper or even Brandon's return to retrieve him?

Could he stomach her hurt when he said what he had to? Or her dismissal? But, come what may, he had to create some much-needed distance. If that required he bring her some amount of pain now in order to avoid greater pain later, so be it.

He sucked in a breath and let it out. And put on all the confidence he could muster. "I cannot in good conscience avoid the issue of your mother."

Sadie blinked. Had she just heard what she thought she had?

David's gaze had an edge of sadness to it. What was that about?

She pushed out a slow breath. "And just what is the issue with my mother?"

He frowned.

And in the space of that breath, her tentatively erected confidence faltered. What would he say? Had she been wrong about him? About his support of her and Mother? She had thought he understood. Was that but a flawed attempt to make a connection? Perhaps he wasn't the ally she had supposed him to be.

"Have you thought about what to do with her?"

Sadie pulled back from him. "What do you mean?"

"She can't stay here forever. How can you tend to her?"

Sadie worked her lower lip between her teeth.

"You can't possibly think you can manage her long term." Even as his words ran over her raw nerves, his voice remained calm and warm. It made this all the more difficult to stomach.

"And just why not?"

"She's...can you not see that she has lost all sense of reality?"

Sadie stood rather abruptly. "No, I do not. She only struggles with the hardship dealt us by Father's duplicity and abandonment."

"She wasn't addled before your father left?"

How could she answer that? It was true that Mother's mind had not been the same over the last couple of years. But it hadn't been as it was now. And so, there was reason to believe it could return to what it had been, wasn't there?

"Mr. Anderson, I think you should leave."

"Sadie, I didn't intend to—"

"Now." She pressed the word out. "Please, Mr. Anderson. Leave now."

"I don't think—"

"Don't make me say it yet again."

He nodded and moved past her toward the door. Why did her body react to the warmth of him as he passed? Traitor.

And it occurred to her that Mr. Miller had dropped him off. What was he supposed to do about that?

"Please, feel free to borrow a horse to get to town. Mr. Miller can return it later." She set her gaze on the floor, refusing to meet his eyes once more.

She sensed that he paused for a moment. Possibly watched her for those few seconds, but then he stepped out of the room.

Curling her fingers into her palms to form fists, she fought the urge to crumple. How could it be that she had lost yet another friend and ally? Was life so cruel?

She closed her eyes. *Lord, what are You doing here? I cannot continue like this.*

But there was silence. No answering peace of spirit. What, after all, had she expected? So tumultuous was her angst that she doubted, even in the quiet, she could sense God. Had He, too, abandoned her? What had she done wrong?

Footfalls just beyond drew nearer. But the sound of the shoes belied the steps were a woman's.

Sadie looked to the door as Aunt Jane appeared. "Is something the matter, dear?"

Drawing in a breath, Sadie closed her eyes again. How could she explain it? Was it even possible to form the words? So, she shook her head.

The swish of skirts told that Aunt Jane entered and came toward her. Could she withstand the kindnesses? Or would it break her?

"Dearest," Aunt Jane said as she paused in front of Sadie, "What happened with your gentleman?"

Her gentleman? Is that what Aunt Jane thought? Why? Had Sadie behaved as such? Had David?

Aunt Jane expelled a sharp breath and set arms around Sadie.

At first, Sadie wanted to fight the gentle embrace, but she found herself unable to. So, she dropped her forehead to Aunt Jane's shoulder. And shook with the torrent of emotion.

Aunt Jane's arms tightened. "It is all right. All will be well."

How could the woman know that? Sadie's world had been upturned. Again. Would it, in fact, work out? For Sadie couldn't see through to the other side.

But she consoled herself with Aunt Jane's care for her and let the tears come.

CHAPTER 13
Ire

David pushed the horse onward a bit harder. Though he knew not why. The horse gave him speed enough for the trip to Wharton City. Was he so desperate to get away from Sadie? Or did he drive so to keep himself from changing his mind?

That thought gave way to a rush of emotion. And he slowed the animal to a gentle trot.

Did he wish to leave her like this? Or should he turn around and make another attempt to clear the air?

Such would only entangle him. And he was fairly certain he didn't want that. No, he had spoken true, and it was up to her to decide how to take it. He had no control over her feelings.

Something whispered in his mind that this wasn't so. Not completely. She had trusted him, opened herself up. And he responded by hurting her. Was that needed?

He turned the horse but halted. Should he go back and try to speak with her? A part of him wanted to. So much.

Yet he knew the stakes: the risk of over-involvement and likely, his heart.

He paused at that thought. Was that so? Had he come to care for her more than he ought?

Shaking his head, he told himself that wasn't the case. He had but softened to her plight. And knew he may be her only hope. That created a feeling of responsibility. As such, he owed her the truth.

He glanced over his shoulder, down the path to Wharton City. Perhaps he might continue. She needed time to discover that he only did what was best.

But the look in her eyes at his words came back to him. And the pain there had stung. Deeply. Was he fooling himself?

The horse shifted beneath him, as if eager for forward momentum.

Yes, the wisest course would be to go on to town, meet up with Brandon, and let things fall where they may. Then why did that decision feel so heavy? And his very being longed to return to the Perkins' estate?

The sound of wagon wheels gave him pause. Someone was headed this way.

He looked in the direction of Wharton City and spotted a horse-drawn cart coming around the bend. Was it Brandon? It appeared so.

Perhaps they might double back to Sadie's and return the horse. And he could ask if she would see him.

David settled and brought the horse to do so as well. And then watched, waiting until his cousin drew closer.

"Whoa," Brandon called as he pulled on the reins. His horse came to a stop several feet short of David. "What are you doing out here? Everything all right?"

How to answer that?

"I...came to find you." There, the simpler, the better.

"On one of the Perkins' horses?"

"Oh. Yes. It's a bit of a story." One he wasn't eager to get into, so he added, "Miss Perkins requested that we return the horse another day."

Brandon nodded. And silence settled between them.

It felt a bit too awkward for David. Was he so out of sorts? "Shall we make our way back to the ranch?"

"Sure." Brandon leaned forward and gripped the reins. Then paused. "Oh...I stopped to check the post. There's a telegram for you, but he wouldn't release it to me."

David was glad to hear it. At least the man adhered to his oath. Not that David had anything to hide from Brandon, but he liked hearing that the telegraph operator wasn't so free with information.

"I suppose I should go and pick it up. It may be important."

Brandon gave him a nod. "Shall we return the horse and then make our way back to Wharton City?"

How could David explain that Sadie likely didn't want to see him for the remainder of the day at least. Perhaps not ever again. That realization pained him more than he would have expected.

"There is no need. Sadie—er, Miss Perkins assured me the horse could be returned tomorrow. I don't wish to keep you from the ranch any more than I already have."

Brandon's brows gathered.

David wasn't doing the best job of making sense out of his decision. But he still wanted to keep what happened between he and Sadie to himself. "I'll ride on into town for that telegram and meet you back at the ranch."

Brandon looked confused and opened his mouth as if to speak.

But David put his heels to the horse's flank and moved off before Brandon could contradict him. And he didn't look back. Nor did he pause again until he came to the office at the end of the main stretch in Wharton City.

He dropped down and secured the horse to the post. Then he dusted himself off. How did anyone keep their garments in presentable form? For certain, he smelled of horse and dirt. It did not please him to realize this.

Still, he did not wish to delay his errand any longer. He had done what he could for the smell. Not that it should matter—everyone here smelled the same as he.

Stepping into the telegraph office, he was relieved to find that no one waited to be helped. So, he strolled to the counter.

The man within sat at a desk, his head and shoulders slumped. Was he asleep?

David coughed.

The man jerked upward, nearly knocking over the chair. Then he glanced about. "Mr. Anderson," he said as he moved toward his side of the counter. "What can I do for you?"

David stifled a grin. "I understand that you have a telegram for me."

"Oh, yes!" The man maneuvered to his stack of papers and sifted through them. Finally pausing and pulling one out. "Here it is."

"Thank you, sir." David took the slip and resisted the urge to read it in that moment but noticed that it was from his father. This may be urgent indeed.

"Any reply?" the man asked, fiddling with his pocket watch.

David scanned the words. His father summoned him home, stating that David's cases called for attention. As well, Father noted that David's absence had extended long enough.

What was he to do? Could he pull out of Sadie's legal matters and return at his father's behest? Perhaps she would dismiss him regardless. Should he, however, make the first move to see that happen?

His heart squeezed and he ignored it. This decision was no place for emotional infringement.

The telegraph operator waited for David's response.

"Yes." David looked up. "I have something to send back."

Sadie looked at the barrel of apples as she walked into the General Store. How many had Mrs. Wallem said she needed? Their supply of things at the house had gotten slim now that Mrs. Wallem was cooking more and there were a couple more mouths to feed.

Picking up one of the red fruits, she examined it. How was one to know a good apple from a bad one? Granted, there wasn't a worm sticking out of it. Even she knew that wasn't one she wanted.

Mrs. Wallem usually did the food purchases. But Sadie had begged to be sent on the errand. There was so much in her head, she welcomed the chance to be out and about and not dwelling on the things David had said. Or didn't say.

That brought a host of questions. What was she to do now? How had she been so wrong about him? Did he ever really care? Or were she and Mother always a means to an end? A way to feel good about his social attentiveness?

Sadie frowned. Here again, she had let her thoughts get away from her. She was supposed to be enjoying a break from all of that.

She grabbed a few apples for her basket and moved farther into the store. The glares of the townsfolk bothered her, but she had come to expect nothing else from them. At least they kept their comments to themselves. Perhaps she should not let words wound her as they did, but it couldn't be helped. Her heart was too tender. Maybe too much for her own good.

A voice near the back of the store in the next aisle caught her attention. She paused. Was that...? How could she have the bad luck to be in the establishment at the same time as the man who had put her to the side?

She peered around the shelf and indeed, there was Josiah speaking with one of the eligible ladies in town. His posture communicated that his interest was more than cordial.

It stung.

But she wondered why it should. It wasn't as if she had truly cared for him. He had, in the end, been but a hope for security. Her heart had not been involved in the arrangement.

Still, her chest tightened, and her face burned. Then it occurred to her—what if he spotted her spying on him? He might just think more of her intrigue.

She spun away and knocked into someone who had been looking at a shelf behind her. Even as Sadie looked up, she bemoaned her tendency of late to pay little mind to her surroundings.

Deputy Travers let out a grunt. Then his eyes lit with recognition. "Watch yourself, Miss Perkins."

Sadie glanced in the direction where Josiah had been standing.

He had gripped the young lady by her elbow and was escorting her away.

Why that should embarrass Sadie, she didn't know, but her face erupted in heat.

"Miss Perkins?" Deputy Travers shifted his weight.

"My apologies. I didn't know you were there."

"That much is clear." He tugged on his vest to straighten it.

"If you'll excuse me." She veered around him and made her way to the counter. Though she had not collected everything on her list, she couldn't stay here any longer.

Setting her basket on the roughened surface, she offered the shopkeeper a small smile as he looked at her wares.

"I...need a sack of flour, too. Oh, and sugar." She struggled to get the words out. Was she so out of sorts?

The man nodded and hefted a sack of each on the counter. "That all?"

"Yes." She wished she had let Mrs. Wallem come. This had been a mistake.

The shopkeeper gave her the total and she paid him.

But as she moved to collect her things—a prospect which promised to be awkward at best, impossible in all likelihood—a man's arms came around the two large sacks.

Deputy Travers.

Had he followed her? Did he not have purchases of his own? That was suspect. What exactly had he been doing when she bumped into him?

"Allow me, Miss Perkins. I'll help you get these things to your wagon."

She paused. Spending another minute in the man's company was not appealing. But she didn't know how to refuse without being rude. Maybe some amount of rudeness was in order.

Still, she could not make the words come out. So, she grabbed her basket and headed outside. Perhaps she could keep well enough away that this would be a brief encounter.

She moved toward her cart, Deputy Travers in tow.

Despite her rapid steps carrying her away from the General Store, his longer stride made it easy for him to keep up with her.

"Where are you off to in such a hurry?" he asked. But he didn't seem to be having even the slightest difficulty.

"These things are needed for the evening's meal. I'm just...eager to get them home." She didn't so much as look in his direction.

"Don't worry your pretty little head about that. I could help you get these things there if you—"

"No," she blurted out, coming to a stop.

He almost dropped the flour sack in his abrupt pause.

"That is," she said, hoping to cover her reaction, "that is kind, but unnecessary, Deputy." She offered a small smile.

"Maybe you need to let people help you more often."

She picked up step again, not knowing how to respond. Was he making an overture?

They made it to the cart in the next few moments—a span in which she avoided his gaze.

He set the sacks in the bed of the cart, giving her a broad grin. "You know, folks around here aren't too keen on you."

She jerked back. Where was he going with this?

"It might help if you were a little...nicer to those that want to help you." He leaned against the side of the wagon. An indication that he didn't plan to let her leave anytime soon?

She wished her emotions weren't always so on display. Her cheeks no doubt showed the reddened evidence that his comment stung. "I'm not sure I catch your meaning."

The deputy tipped his hat to a couple passing by. "See that? They don't appear too interested in even a simple greeting for you."

Sadie frowned. Could she not just be on her way?

He stepped closer. "I wouldn't be in a hurry to discourage anyone who might be less than cold, if I were you." As he spoke, he set a hand next to hers near the basket.

She pulled her hand back, but he grabbed for it.

"I could be very helpful in that regard." He looked into her eyes.

It made her more than a little uncomfortable. She wasn't sure she liked what he was insinuating. Much less the crawling of her skin at his attention.

"Folks like me. They respect me. Trust my opinion."

She wasn't sure that was quite true. But the whole conversation was headed in a bad direction. Jerking her hand free, she narrowed her gaze. "I'm quite certain the townsfolk will come around."

Sadie stepped to the side to go around him and to the front of the cart.

"That ain't all." He moved into her path. "With all this...legal trouble you are in, a man to put his name on whatever you have left, might ease things a bit."

She widened her eyes. Dare he be so bold? "I appreciate your concern, Deputy, but I think we'll be fine."

"We? You and that strange case of a mother? And just how is she gonna help you out?"

Sadie drew in a breath. "Mr. Travers, I really must be on my way." She tried to get around him once more.

He grabbed her arm. "If I were you, I wouldn't be so dismissive."

She seethed. "Turn me loose."

He glared down at her as if he dared her to defy him.

"Turn me loose or I'll scream."

"Now that would be a show." But he let go his hold. "Just think about what I said. It might be your best hope. I certainly wouldn't put any faith in some fancy lawyer whose words are fine, but his follow through isn't."

She turned her back on him and pulled herself up onto the driver's bench. "Don't get caught in the wheels." Grabbing for the reins, she added, "You might not find it so pleasant."

He stepped back as she urged her horse onward. And, folding his arms across his chest, he watched her go.

She let out a breath. How dare he be so forward! He had no right... no right in the least.

If that were true, then why did her insides shake? Was there truth to his words? And if not, why did she turn the horse toward the Miller Ranch?

CHAPTER 14

Connection

David watched the painted mare in its stall. He had yet to understand why it was in the barn rather than the paddock just outside. How did the ranchers determine when a horse was inside or outside? Perhaps the horses were out as needed for use or exercise. Maybe this mare was injured or recovering.

There was little reason to waste thought on it. The chance he would work it out was small. But he remained and eyed the animal. It was an admirable creature. So useful, utilitarian maybe, but interesting to look at.

The animal had come to the stall door and seemed to be watching *him*. Did the creature have deep thoughts? Or any thoughts about him? It could be that the horse only hoped for a bit of something to eat. Yes, that was likely it.

Movement at the opening to the barn drew his attention. A feminine figure stood silhouetted against the midday sun streaming in.

"David?" It was Amanda's voice.

"Yes. I'm here." Why was he a little put out to be found admiring the mare? Would it ruin their opinion of him? Interfere with his status as an indifferent observer in all things about the ranch? Did it even matter?

She strode toward him. "I didn't know where you had gone."

He supposed that was true. It wasn't like he frequented the barn. The whole place had a wild, yet earthy smell to it. The sweat of the men, mingled with that of the animals and their...by products...was not inviting. Yet here he stood, taking it in.

"I needed to...think," he admitted. Then chided himself. Why had he told her that?

Now she was at his side, turned toward the horse. She lifted a hand to the animal's face and rubbed it between the eyes. The thing must be filthy! Still, he found his own fingers itching to do the same. What was this place doing to him?

David shifted to the side. "What can I do for you?" Had Amanda come looking for him? Or on some other errand?

"Oh," she said as she slapped her hands together and then wiped them against her apron, "I was looking for Brandon. Have you seen him?"

"Not for some time. I think I heard him about an hour ago in the paddock."

She glanced toward the barn opening. "He's not there now."

"Is there something I can help with?"

She shook her head. "No, I'll just wait until he comes in for lunch." Then her gaze returned to the horse.

He wasn't certain how to proceed, so he asked one of the many questions that had plagued him as he stood here. "What is the horse's name?"

"Ty."

"Ty?" It sounded more a masculine name. Oh well, if people insisted on naming the creatures, why not have it be interesting?

She nodded. "Samuel's first horse."

That made more sense. A gentler horse, but the lad perhaps had wished for a boy horse. "How old was he?"

"Eight. Brandon was pleased to secure him a horse, but I had... rather mixed feelings."

"Oh?" That didn't seem remarkably young.

"You can probably imagine how uneasy I was with the idea. I might have been a little overprotective."

"Aren't all mothers?" David again felt the urge to touch the horse but fought it. He didn't need dirt and animal filth smeared on his hands.

"I suppose." She crossed her arms and continued watching the horse.

"Why is Ty in the barn instead of the paddock?" He ventured to secure an answer to another wondering.

Amanda looked to him; her eyes lit up. "She is about to be a mother herself."

"Oh." David tried to eye the horse's midsection. Indeed, there was a marked swell there. How had he missed it? Then again, he wasn't overly acquainted with these things. "How soon?"

"Any day now." Amanda smiled again. "Samuel is over the moon. Brandon said he could help with the..." Her words trailed off.

He was about to ask if she was all right when he heard it—the gentle thundering of hoofbeats.

"Perhaps Brandon," David said. "I'll let you—"

"Shh!" she commanded, holding up a hand. "That's a horse and cart."

How could she tell that from such a distance? But he hadn't the chance to ask before she moved off.

He followed, a bit concerned. The ranch was not often graced with company. Certainly not unexpected visitors. Picking up step, he joined Amanda at the wide opening and he looked to the far side of the dirt road.

Sure enough, there was a cart there. And it approached at an alarming speed.

"Should we be concerned?" He glanced about for any sign of the ranch hands.

"It's Sadie," Amanda gasped.

Sadie? How could Amanda possibly know that? But as he watched, the cart drew nearer and the figure in the driver's seat...well, it could be Sadie. Though he couldn't be sure.

Did he want it to be Sadie? His heart thumped hard as if to the beat of the hooves clomping against the path. Was he ready to face her? Had she come to dismiss him? Or tell him what was what?

There was no way to know.

Amanda stepped out from the shade of the barn and called to the side.

One of the ranch hands—the one with the younger face—came around and strode toward Amanda. David wondered if he should step forward to receive Sadie? Or fall back into shadow until he could understand more?

But as Sadie neared, he became certain that she was in some manner of distress and he found himself unable to maintain a distance. He had to know. So, he stepped out of the barn and by the time the cart slowed to a halt, David was just behind Amanda.

"Sadie," Amanda said as she stepped to the horse. She rested a hand on the horse—this time to its neck. "Are you well?"

Sadie heaved as if physically exerted. Or emotionally overwhelmed. Either way, he wanted to know. Needed to know.

"Come, let us get you somewhere more comfortable." Amanda and the ranch hand moved toward Sadie.

The rancher lifted his arms to help Sadie down.

Why was David upset by that? The man's hands about Sadie's waist did not appear intrusive or pressing. And when he set her to the ground, he kept an arm's length of space between them. Nothing untoward.

Still, it bothered David.

Amanda moved to Sadie's side and set an arm about her shoulders. "You need a glass of water. Let's get you out of this heat."

Urging Sadie in the direction of the homestead brought them by David.

Sadie glanced at him, her eyes catching on his. Hers were reddened, maybe even swollen. From the amount of dirt kicked up in her rush? Or from something that bothered her?

Amanda continued walking her past David. She spoke soothing words to Sadie that he couldn't catch. Indeed, in that moment, the world became muffled. He froze to the spot. Had he caused this?

He watched the two women pass and move on toward the porch.

"You all right, Mr. Anderson?" the baby-faced ranch hand asked, looking over his shoulder as he grabbed the horse's bit.

David nodded and turned to follow Amanda and Sadie.

He didn't catch up with them until they were inside and Amanda was settling Sadie at the dining table.

"Cook," Amanda yelled.

There was no answer. Where was the woman? The normal clatter of pots and whatnot was absent.

"She must be hanging the laundry." Amanda crossed the room. "I'll get you that water."

And then she pushed the door open and disappeared, leaving him and Sadie alone. His gaze was then glued to her, but she wouldn't look up from the tabletop.

"Sadie, I...didn't want to distress you so."

She shook her head.

"Believe me, it was never my intention to—"

"It's not you." Her words were quiet, but curt. "So, you can let yourself off the hook."

"Let myself off the...?" He could barely form the words. "Sadie, it's not—"

Amanda stepped into the room, glass in hand. She set it in front of Sadie and took the seat beside her. As Sadie took a sip, Amanda put a hand to Sadie's shoulder. "You want to talk about it?"

David frowned, but his every sense was trained on Sadie.

He barely noticed Amanda toss a look in his direction. Did she think he should leave? Not a chance. Something had upset Sadie, and he needed to know what.

"I..." Sadie drew in a ragged breath. "I didn't know where to go. I can't let my...my mother and Aunt Jane see me like this. And I don't have anyone—"

"You came to the right place," Amanda interjected. "You are always welcome here."

Had Sadie come because he was here? Or because Amanda was? Had she sought him out despite their earlier interaction?

"Want to tell me what happened?" Amanda prompted.

Sadie nodded, her breath catching. As if there were tears forthcoming.

It stabbed at him.

"Just..." Amanda rubbed her shoulder. "...start at the beginning."

Sadie sucked in a breath and let it out slowly. Then she spoke. "I was at the General Store. Mrs. Wallem needed some foodstuffs."

Amanda nodded, encouraging.

David felt as if he were invisible, but he didn't speak up to prove the contrary, and he would not leave until he knew what had upset Sadie.

"I must have bumped into Deputy Travers. He..." Sadie paused and seemed to rethink her words. "I'm not sure if he was following me or just shopping for something nearby."

Something hot formed in the pit of David's stomach.

"Anyway, I apologized and purchased my things. Then, the deputy insisted on walking me to my cart."

David did not like where this was going.

Amanda maintained a calm demeanor. "Then what happened?"

Did Amanda not suspect what was coming? How could she not?

"And he...said that no one cared. That if I wanted to find a way out of this mess, I would do well to consider him an option."

"Oh?" Amanda kept her voice level. But David noticed that the hand she kept away from Sadie had formed a fist.

Indeed, his own palms ached from his fingers curling tightly into them. How dare the man presume such? And insinuate that Sadie needed him to rescue her? That she had no other options. Of course, she did. There were plenty of...

Only there weren't.

Still, it angered David that the deputy would take advantage of the situation. He wouldn't allow it. His hands ached to make contact with Deputy Travers in some way...to hit him, to make sure he never dared so much as approach Sadie again.

Sadie was not friendless. And he would not allow her to be hopeless.

A cry pierced the air.

David glanced about. What was that?

"I need to get that," Amanda said.

Was it the toddler then? Oh yes, he usually napped until lunch time.

"But I will be back shortly." Amanda rose and gave David a meaningful look. A warning of sorts?

As Amanda stepped from the room, Sadie wrapped her arms around herself. And shook.

Was she cold? That couldn't be. It was rather warm in here.

But he came around the table and swallowing his ire, sat in the seat Amanda had vacated. Sadie needed his support, not his anger.

"Sadie," he said softly. More softly than he would have thought possible.

She sniffled but did not look at him.

He pressed a hand to her arm.

Her trembling increased.

Without pausing to consider his actions, he pulled her into his embrace. She leaned into him, grabbing his shirt. And pressed her face to his chest.

"Sadie, I will not let you be so desperate."

She quieted.

"I will do everything necessary to keep you and your mother safe. You are not alone in this."

She whimpered.

He moved a hand between them and tilted her chin up with his fingers. Then he was looking into her eyes.

She seemed so lost, but there was a glimmer of hope in there. Because of him? Because of his words?

He could no more deny the urge to lean forward than he could stop his heart from beating. And the desire to communicate everything he felt—the overwhelming protectiveness that had come over him, his ache for her hurt, and his care for her—filled him.

And he claimed her lips.

Sadie settled into David as his mouth slanted onto hers.

Her first kiss. And it was bliss.

She hadn't even known she craved to be in his arms until she was.

As his lips moved over hers, the kiss became possessive and wanting. As if he, too, craved more of her. Was this how it was supposed to be?

Her head swam and she gripped his shoulders to stay grounded to the moment. If not, she would certainly float away.

One moment he pressed into her, the next he pulled back.

She almost protested, but the absence of his warmth took her breath away. Opening her eyes, she tried to steady herself yet again as the room spun.

"David?" His name slipped out without warning.

His hands moved on her arms. She hadn't realized they were still about her.

Sadie closed her eyes and leaned toward him once more, but his hands, once gentle, firmed and maintained the distance between their bodies. Why?

"Sadie," he rasped, his voice sounded as unsteady as she felt.

Her fingers grasped his arms even as the muscles under her hands tightened. She needed to feel him, to know that he was real. The last several moments had seemed dreamlike.

"Sadie," he said more clearly. Or was it that she heard more clearly now as the fog surrounding her brain dissipated? "Sadie, we... shouldn't."

That jerked her to reality. Did he regret kissing her? Her eyes widened as her heart bore the brunt of his words.

"No." His eyes searched hers, his mouth a thin line.

Was that an answer to her unspoken question? Or another insistence that they not continue this?

"I...want to." One of his hands rose and touched the side of her face ever so lightly. "But it is not proper."

The sharp ache in her chest eased. He did have a care.

She slid a hand to the collar of his shirt, still wanting...needing the connection with him.

He shifted and grunted as her fingers grazed the skin at his neck. And he captured her hand in his, tugging it down so that the fabric of his shirt was more solidly between their skin.

She couldn't help but study his eyes, his features, his movements...so caught up in him. Did he feel the same?

In the next minute, however, he leaned farther back. That broke the spell that seemed to swirl around them.

What was this—something rash or the culmination of what had been building between them? And what did it mean? Did he care for her? Deeply enough to abandon his earlier reservations?

Movement near the great room stirred her even more. Sadie watched as first David looked in that direction, then her gaze followed his.

Amanda stood at the edge of the dining space, a young child in her arms. Her expression was unreadable. But if Sadie had to guess, she would say the woman was not overly pleased.

David pulled away even more, until they no longer had any physical contact. Was he embarrassed? Ashamed? A pang shot through her core.

Amanda eyed him. "I apologize...for interrupting."

"Nonsense," David said as he stood.

Would he deny what had happened here? Could Sadie bear that?

"I...should see if Brandon has returned from the pasture." He ran a hand through his hair.

Did she imagine it, or did he seem a little shaken? But by what? The kiss? Or perhaps that Amanda suspected it?

Sadie had little opportunity to discern his true feelings before he turned and moved to the door.

As odd as it was, she wanted something more from him. Some sort of recognition of what had happened. And a reason to hope it meant something.

He opened the door and her heart dropped.

But he paused and looked back at her.

For a moment, she believed he would apologize. That would indeed destroy her.

As his gaze settled on hers, the warmth of his affection poured between her shoulder blades. Yes, he did care. She was certain of it.

He opened his mouth, then closed it. Was it so difficult for him to form a sentence?

Her face heated.

"We'll talk soon." The words came with more confidence than he appeared to have. Then he stepped outside, and the door clattered closed behind him.

All the tension in Sadie released. Would she slide from the chair? Her body relaxed into the renewed hope his words had offered. As much as a part of her charged with excitement at the notion of being alone with him again.

Footfalls warned that Amanda moved. She came around the table and sat in the already pulled out chair just vacated. The youngster squealed in delight as he patted his hands together.

Amanda cleared her throat. "I don't know what—"

The door from the kitchen slammed open, and Cook stepped into the room.

"Goodness gracious! I am late getting them vittles on the table." The older woman bustled about, checking the table and the sideboard. "My apologies. I'll have them out soon enough."

Cook nodded at Sadie, only then seeming to notice she was there. "Good day, Miss Perkins. I—oh no, is something wrong?"

Wrong?

Then Sadie remembered. She had been crying. The evidence was likely all over her face—puffy eyes, drawn features.

"No, ma'am, I am quite well." Sadie looked to Cook but shot a quick glance to Amanda, who seemed rather humored by the situation.

"Good." Cook nodded. "I best get that food going." She turned and stepped back into the kitchen. The sound of pots and pans filled the space.

Sadie looked back at Amanda, but only briefly. She was not looking forward to hearing from this fine woman that there was anything untoward in David's manner or behavior. How could Sadie regret that kiss and the way the very thought of it still brought every nerve to life?

"I don't think—" Amanda started again. But the sounds from the kitchen became louder, drowning out her words.

Pausing, Amanda offered Sadie a smile. "I think we might as well see if we can help in there."

Sadie let out a breath, letting the rest of her tension go. Perhaps, then, their conversation could wait. The longer the better. For Sadie needed to get a handle on what she was feeling. And thinking. Maybe then she could express it to someone else. Maybe.

CHAPTER 15
Hope Renewed

Sadie set the last plate on the table. It wasn't so long ago that this very thing would be unthinkable. Back when her father would have insisted she not stoop so low, that there were those in the home whose job it was to do such things.

But everything had changed. And she wasn't under Father's thumb anymore.

Besides, a job well done, such as setting the table, gave her a sense of satisfaction.

Just beyond the door, the clomping of several sets of boots against the boards of the front porch echoed. Seems she finished just in time.

She should inquire if Cook and Amanda had anything else for her to do. Yet she found herself unable to move from the spot. Turning toward the door, she prepared to greet the hungry menfolk. One of which she was most eager to set eyes on.

The door opened and her heart did a little flip. Was David about to enter? How would he behave toward her? Surely, that would be telling of his true feelings.

In came the ranch hands, all of them. With Mr. Miller, who tipped his head to her as he removed his hat.

She smiled but couldn't resist looking around the group to spy if

David were just behind them. But he wasn't. Where could he be? Hadn't he gone to find Mr. Miller? Why, then, was *he* here, but not David?

Her heart thumped harder. And with it, she grimaced. Because of the added aching sensation? Or due to her disappointment?

Would David not come? Was he so put out that he wouldn't even face Sadie?

The men took their seats, but Sadie couldn't make herself move.

More footfalls and voices beyond the door drew her attention once more. Perhaps she had become dismayed prematurely.

Sure enough, in came Samuel and David. They chatted, but their voices halted as they entered.

David's gaze met Sadie's. And the world stopped.

Her face warmed and she grinned.

The edges of his mouth teased upward but did not spread. He didn't appear pleased to see her. Nor was he upset exactly. What went on in that head of his?

"Please, have a seat," Amanda said from behind Sadie. When had she come into the room?

Looking to her friend, Sadie saw that Amanda's arm had stretched out, indicating the chair just in front of where they stood.

Sadie offered a weak smile and sat.

But then, David slipped around those still standing to take the seat beside her. Was he eager to sit next to her? Maybe she shouldn't read too much into his earlier expression.

Mr. Miller's mother came from the direction of the hall, their daughter Lucy in tow, and the toddler Amanda had held earlier on her hip.

Everyone settled into their places, though the table did seem a little crowded. Still, they all sat and awaited whatever Cook had prepared for them. The food smelled delicious...some sort of chicken dish by the scent.

The din of voices surrounded Sadie, but all she could think about was how close David's arm was to hers. They were almost brushing. Yet not.

Mr. Miller raised his voice. "Everyone, now that you have your seats..."

The volume in the room lowered at his behest.

"...let's return thanks."

Amanda had sat down next to her husband and now reached over to slip her hand into his.

Mr. Miller, in turn, gripped her fingers and bowed his head. Then he lifted up words of gratitude and thanksgiving.

Sadie wished she could follow his words better, but it was difficult.

A warm hand slid over hers in her lap. David? She knew it was by the way his touch brought a tingle to her whole being. He squeezed her hand as the prayer continued. What was he trying to communicate? Whatever his intention, it gave her renewed hope.

Why did she constantly doubt him? Because she had been abandoned too many times in these last weeks? That was not his fault. And it wasn't fair to put it off on him. She needed to trust in the fact that he stayed by her side—even when she pushed him away—and believe that something was blooming here.

The prayer ended and, though everyone resumed their conversations, David did not release her hand. Instead, he rubbed a thumb along her fingers. What was he doing to her?

Cook brought in a large bowl of chicken and dumplings. The aroma soothed and warmed Sadie's senses. And her mouth watered.

David's hand slipped from its hold on hers.

The meal commenced with servings and the clatter of silverware.

"Miss Perkins?"

Sadie tore her attention away from her food and looked to where the voice had come from. It was Mr. Miller's mother. "Yes?"

"It is so good to have you join us. I have heard good things about you."

Sadie fought the urge to glance at David. Was he sharing things with his family? What kinds of things? Good? Or things she would rather keep private?

Regardless, she returned the pleasantries. "Thank you, ma'am. I...do what I can."

A strange look crossed over the woman's features, but she shifted her focus downward to her plate.

That did not ease Sadie's confusion. Or concern.

As if sensing her uneasiness, David's hand covered hers once more.

She chanced a glance at him.

His gaze was on her, but he soon attended to his meal as well. But this time, he did not remove his hold.

Conversations continued around the table, but Sadie found it difficult to focus on anything. And so, the meal passed without any further disruption. Until...

"Did you secure passage for your return?" Mr. Miller said from farther away.

Who was he talking to? Someone planned a trip? But as she looked to him, she found his gaze set on David.

She jerked her regard to David as well. Was he leaving?

He gripped her hand tighter.

But she yanked away. The movement was big enough to gain notice.

Her features heated. And she blotted her mouth with her napkin. Perhaps anyone who saw would dismiss it as her gathering the cloth. Little chance of that. And her fears were confirmed by the looks she garnered.

She coughed. And couldn't stop.

"Are you all right?" Amanda's hand patted her arm.

Sadie nodded and reached for her water. But that did nothing to calm the coughs. Or her skittering heartbeat. What was this? David planned to leave and did not so much as mention it?

"Please, excuse me," Sadie managed to get out. She rose and rushed around the table and out the front door. Where she was headed, she didn't know. She needed air, and space to think. And feel.

Stepping outside proved not enough, however. She ran down the porch stairs and into the field beyond. Going as fast as her legs could carry her. Could she reach a place where she was safe? Would she ever be?

David glanced around the table at the surprised expressions. What would everyone think if he went after Sadie? Did it matter?

"Excuse me." He stood and dropped his napkin on the table. Then, pressing down his concern for the opinions around him, he walked to the door, as calmly as humanly possible, and slipped outside.

A brief relief rushed over him as he left the stares behind. But he looked around for Sadie. She wasn't on the porch. Where had she gone?

He scanned the area.

There.

She ran from the homestead as if the devil himself chased her. Is that what he was in this moment? The devil to her angel?

He lengthened his stride and followed.

It took longer than he'd have liked to catch up to her. And he was sucking in air by the time he did so. As he neared her now stopped figure, he wondered what he would say. How could he repair this mess? He wanted to more than ease her heart and make everything all right. His concern for her was too deep for him to believe that. He needed to help her understand.

"Sadie," he said as he drew to a stop. He scanned the area and let the scent of wildflowers soothe him as he pulled in more air than normal.

She stared at the pond in front of her. But her shoulders shook. Was she crying? If so, why wasn't she making a sound?

He stepped next to her and set eyes on her face at last.

The sight of her tears cut through him. And he wanted to pull her to his chest. But he couldn't. That wouldn't be right.

"Sadie, I was planning to tell you."

"That you were leaving? Did you plan to tell me before? Or write me after?"

He looked to the ground. This wasn't going to be pleasant. "Before. It just...it all happened so fast."

She set a hard gaze on him. "I'm sorry it has been so difficult for you." Then she turned away as the shaking of her body intensified.

"That's not what I meant. My father...he sent a telegram. I am needed in Richmond."

She nodded. Did she really understand? Because he wasn't sure he would in her position. "Why then?"

"Why what?" he asked, as if he didn't know. He had been wrong in his displays of affection.

"Why did you...kiss me?" She continued to look in the opposite direction. Would this be better if she met his gaze? Or harder?

He swallowed. If he'd had any wits about him in that moment he had pressed his lips to hers, he would have stopped it before he... But he had lost control of himself. His care for her was too great, and her need of him had driven him to a rash action. Now he had wounded her.

And that was the last thing he wanted to do.

"It seemed..." He paused. "The other day...it seemed you didn't want to have anything to do with me. After...what I said."

She sniffled, wiping at the tears on her cheeks. Her hair whipped in the wind. Indeed, the breeze would have been soothing had he the thought to enjoy it. Instead, he was caught up in this tense moment. As it was his gaze—and his heart—were set on her.

"Sadie, I can send a message to my father." Did he truly believe that? Or was he only trying to make this better? "Tell him I am needed here..."

She whirled around. "Don't go doing me any favors." Her words were sharp.

"I...that's not what I meant." He looked down as he kicked at the dirt. Then faced her again. "I made a commitment to you. And I want to honor that."

She let out a gasp, then appeared to gather herself. "Is that all? A commitment?"

He wanted to kick himself. This was coming out all wrong. Was there any semblance of a path through this? Was he prepared to share his heart with her? "No. That's not all. I—"

"I release you from your...commitment. Have a safe trip back to Richmond." She turned and headed back toward the homestead.

"Sadie, that's not what I meant. I—"

"I can't do this anymore," she said as she turned and shook her head. "It's too hard."

He bit his lip. How could he have hurt her like this? His own chest became a cavern, thick with heat. Maybe she was right. This was too hard.

She spun and continued back to the house.

And he let his gaze settle on the rippling of the water in the breeze. Some things just were. That was all.

CHAPTER 16

Leaving

Sadie pulled on the horse's reins as she neared the fine house. She was relieved to be home. It wasn't much of a release, as there were challenges here, too, but there wasn't that same tension she had just endured. That had been difficult. She would not let it hold her back.

Yes, there had been a hope with David. Yes, she had counted on him. But it wasn't right to have leaned on him so heavily. Had this business with Father, and then Josiah, not taught her better than that?

She would learn. Perhaps she had finally.

As she maneuvered the horse and cart, and the other mare David had borrowed, toward the barn, she noticed that another horse stood near the front door, munching on grass.

Who had come? Would it be David—to try and make amends again? She couldn't take that. But that was rather doubtful. How would he have traveled another way and made it here before she had?

Concern fell over her and she only settled the horse, tying the reins off on the nearby post. Her need to find out was too great to take the time to put the horses and cart away properly. They would keep.

Rushing for the door as quickly as she could, she flung the obstacle to the side. A little too forcefully. The hinges groaned and squealed at her treatment. She cared not.

"Mrs. Wallem?" she called as she entered. The house was a bit too quiet. "Aunt Jane?"

The stand and plant that always sat by the base of the stairs had toppled over. Had something bad happened here? Or did it merely get bumped? Her heart pumped hard.

Footfalls landed on the wooden floor at the far end of the house. Someone came toward her. There was little reason to remain and wait, so Sadie moved in the direction of the sound.

She intercepted Mrs. Wallem.

"Sadie, thank the Lord you are home."

That didn't ease Sadie's racing thoughts.

Mrs. Wallem took a breath and set hands on Sadie's arm. "Your mother had a fall."

What had happened? Thick fear rose into her throat. "A fall?"

Mrs. Wallem nodded.

"What happened?" It was difficult to get the words out. The world around her became a little off kilter.

"It's best you speak with Dr. Norwood, I—"

"Dr. Norwood?" The climbing sense of foreboding grabbed a hold of Sadie completely. She could hardly see straight. "Mrs. Wallem, what happened to my mother?"

The older woman first appeared as if she would dismiss Sadie's beseeching and insist upon the doctor. But she let out a breath and relented. "Your mother slipped on the stairs, but she—"

Panic gripped Sadie. "The stairs? How did she get on the stairs?" They had moved Mother into a room down here so she wouldn't be negotiating the stairs.

"We left her sleeping. For only a few moments. We are not sure why she attempted the stairs. She had been calling for you. Maybe she went looking for..."

Mrs. Wallem urged Sadie toward the back of the house as she continued. But her words were drowned out with the thudding of Sadie's heartbeat, now in her ears. This was all *her* fault. Mother had wanted her. And she had lingered at the Miller Ranch for her own selfish reasons. It wasn't right. Sadie hated herself for it.

The kind woman who had been through much with Sadie led her back to Mother's room. They stepped within.

Dr. Norwood spoke with a rather upset Aunt Jane. Mother was abed across the room, sleeping soundly.

As Sadie entered, their conversation let up. And their eyes landed on Sadie.

Aunt Jane appeared rather distraught. She had clearly been crying.

Dr. Norwood frowned and what lines there were in his young features deepened. He strode toward Sadie. And, setting a hand to her elbow, said, "Let's speak in the parlor."

Sadie's gaze was on Mother's form.

Dr. Norwood held up an arm to usher her out of the room.

She didn't want to go. Didn't want to hear whatever he had to say... and yet she did. And needed to. So, she relented and let the doctor urge her down the hall.

When they entered, she paused. Dr. Norwood halted a few steps ahead of her. "Shall we sit?"

"No. Tell me what's going on with my mother."

His eyes were kind as he said, "I really think we should sit."

Mrs. Wallem nodded and gently pressed Sadie further into the parlor.

Sadie allowed it and soon settled herself on the edge of her favorite settee.

Dr. Norwood sat on a chair opposite her.

"I'll get some tea," Mrs. Wallem said before turning and abandoning Sadie.

She hadn't known how much she wanted Mrs. Wallem to stay until the woman walked out of the room. Forcing her regard to the doctor, Sadie braced herself as best she could.

"I don't know what Mrs. Wallem has told you. But your mother fell down several stairs."

Sadie nodded, the movement somewhat tentative.

"She shouldn't be on the stairs in her condition." The doctor's words were flat.

"Yes, that's why we moved her from her bedchambers to this room."

The doctor nodded. "Then it's an issue of attending to her properly."

Sadie bit at her lip. She knew he was right, but what more could they do? Aunt Jane couldn't stay forever.

"I understand that this is quite impossible. And impractical."

Sadie nodded. How could she otherwise? They had done what they could and had failed.

"So, I think it's time you consider the asylum."

Sadie jerked her gaze to him. That wasn't an option. Never.

"I can see you are just as opposed as you have been. And I understand. But you can no longer care for your mother appropriately. Not all the time. It's just not feasible. These institutions...while challenged... have the proper set up to safely manage someone in your mother's condition."

He paused. Did he do so to let his words sink in?

Sadie was tempted to let the burning in the pit of her stomach rise and become a flare of anger. But she couldn't. Dr. Norwood only said what he thought was best. But he wasn't right, was he?

"You know it's true." His words were gentle.

Sadie bit at her lip to keep her emotion from spilling out.

"It was a bad sprain this time. Next time it could be much worse. Are you willing to risk that?" His tone remained kind, but his expression was harder. As if he spoke to a child.

She couldn't bear one more person's ridicule. Not today. "I thank you for your assistance. And for your advice."

"But..." he prompted.

She chewed at her lip. "I have much to think on."

He sighed. "I am not surprised to hear you say that. I expected nothing else." He stood and gathered his bag. "But I do urge you to consider it. Things will only become more dire here."

She rose. "Thank you, doctor." That was all she could manage with her swirling thoughts.

He nodded. "Tell Mrs. Wallem I am sorry I can't stay for tea. I'd best get back to the clinic."

Sadie stepped forward to follow him to the door.

He held up a hand. "I'll see myself out. You take this time to think on what I've said."

She wanted to appease him but found herself unable to even nod in that moment.

And he didn't wait. He maneuvered out of the parlor and disappeared into the hall.

Sadie fell back onto the settee. Was there no rest for the weary? No solace for her spirit? She wanted to ask the Lord these questions but found herself unable to lift the lightest inquiry to heaven as her struggles had only intensified. Perhaps her faith wasn't strong enough to weather these storms.

David grimaced as the wagon pulled to a stop in front of the telegraph office. This was it. He was going home. For better or for worse.

Brandon hopped out of the cart. Was he so eager to see his cousin go? After helping his wife and then his mother down, he moved to the back and began setting the luggage on the platform.

David, too, found his way to the ground and came around to join Brandon.

At first, Brandon looked surprised, but then smiled as David grabbed for one of Aunt Sylvia's bags. How long ago had they been here, loading these things? Not that David had helped his cousin. He had been too...what? Too worried about sullying his clothes? It seemed strange now. Although one of the things he would not miss about this place was the smell. And the constant film of dirt over everything.

But he would miss a few things...or rather, he would miss a few people. That brought an unwelcome pang. He ached to see Sadie one more time. To touch her, or better yet—assure himself that she would be well.

How strange that he came so far, escaping Claire's rejection, and found himself at the end of another kind of dismissal. One that hurt far worse than anything Claire did or said. Ever.

Aunt Sylvia spoke with Amanda, but as David watched, she excused herself to wander to the General Store. They had arrived in Wharton

City with plenty of time to spare. Indeed, the stagecoach hadn't yet arrived to load them.

So, he didn't worry a bit about Aunt Sylvia's little jaunt.

David nodded at Brandon as he grabbed the last of the luggage pieces. Now everything he and Aunt Sylvia had traveled with sat at the ready. It didn't feel real that they had been here a couple of months. Quite a bit longer than David had anticipated. Yet he knew he would choose to stay if he could and try to mend the hurt he visited upon Sadie.

There was no cause to dwell on this. He had to focus on now...and what was ahead. The stage would be here within the hour, and he would leave Wharton City behind for good. Well, at least if he had anything to say about it. He did wonder if Amanda and Brandon would wait to see him and Aunt Sylvia off or would they bid their farewells and return to the ranch?

Stepping to Amanda's side, he noted that Brandon had become caught up in conversation with a man unknown to David. With all the time spent on the ranch, Brandon and Amanda likely enjoyed the opportunities afforded them to engage with their neighbors and fellow townsfolk.

David couldn't help but think of the townspeople in light of how they had treated Sadie. Their stares and muttered comments. It did not endear them to him.

"Looking for someone?" Amanda's words, though gentle, still stung.

He met her gaze. "No. Just...taking it in one last time."

Amanda's mouth became a thin line. "You don't have to go, you know."

That gave him pause. Was Amanda so bold?

"I didn't intend to intrude." She watched him. Did she gauge his reaction? "But I can't help but wonder if this is the right thing."

David sighed. How much to go into this with Amanda? He had no desire to rehash everything. If he were honest with himself, however, he had known this conversation was coming from the moment Amanda had walked in to find him and Sadie kissing.

"At the very least you promised to help Sadie with her legal troubles."

David nodded. "I had every desire to follow through. But she dismissed me. Said she didn't need—or want—my help. Not anymore." He let his gaze wander to the townsfolk again. And tried to not let the presence of the wound in his heart show on his features.

"She was angry," Amanda said, shifting. "Surely you can understand that."

"I...don't know what else to do. This was never supposed to be even this long of a trip. I am needed at the law firm."

"That's just an excuse, and you know it," Amanda shot back, though her tone retained its tenderness. As if she sympathized with him.

"That *is* bold, Mrs. Miller."

"Pardon me. As I said, it was not my intention to overstep."

He nodded. Wishing for Brandon's company for once.

"Perhaps it is best you go." Amanda looked toward the end of the main stretch as if she could conjure the stage.

He tilted his head. Had he heard her correctly? What brought about such a change of opinion?

"After all, if you're not willing to risk anything, you don't deserve her." Amanda brushed past him. "Pardon me." Then she stepped to where Brandon was, still chatting with the stranger. She slipped a hand around Brandon's arm and moved closer.

Even that brought a deepening to David's ache. Was Amanda right? How could he stay and preserve his heart? It had been impossible as it was to keep proper distance from Sadie. And she had made it clear that she didn't need him anymore.

"Well, if it isn't Mr. Anderson!" a higher pitched voice called from behind, in the direction of the telegraph office.

He turned. Sure enough, there stood Miss Alice Higgins, grinning like a cat eyeing a canary. Still, he offered her a smile he didn't feel. "Good day, Miss Higgins."

"Good day to you, too. I did not expect to run across anyone I would recognize on my little trip to this forsaken place."

He understood all too well. Hadn't he had the same thoughts not so long ago?

She sauntered up to him. "I understand that you are on your way back to Richmond."

"Yes, as a fact, I am."

She eyed the luggage piled nearby. "I am sad to see you go. There is so little culture about this place. And it will be all the more lacking as you leave."

He nodded, but his mind wandered. The urge to ask after Sadie was great. Then it occurred to him that someone had to get Miss Higgins to town. Sadie might even be here, about to appear at any moment.

"How is Miss Perkins?" he ventured, hoping to gain the information he sought.

"Oh, she is the same as ever. She is at the house, guarding her mother."

"Guarding her mother?"

"You know, she is sitting with her mother. Watching her. That woman requires constant supervision now."

"Constant supervision? Really?" That wasn't as he remembered it.

"Oh, you didn't know? The poor thing fell down the stairs a couple of days ago while Sadie was out of the house. About killed herself."

"My goodness." David's heart tugged at him. Was Sadie all right? She couldn't have taken that news well.

Miss Higgins shrugged. "If Sadie insists on keeping Aunt Eugenia out of the madhouse, she needs to take better care."

David frowned. Indeed, he wished to naysay Miss Higgins. To give her a little perspective. But he doubted it would do any good. And it would only further involve him in matters he had been invited to see his way out of.

"Perhaps," Miss Higgins said, breaking his concentration as she moved a step closer, "I might find my way out to Richmond in the near future." She batted eyes at him in that annoying way females did when on the prowl.

David's collar became too tight all of a sudden.

"I do so enjoy traveling." Her mouth slanted in a smile that seemed quite a bit more.

Miss Higgins was fairly attractive. And he had never been one to turn away from feminine attentions. But this seemed...out of place. It felt wrong. As if he somehow would be betraying Sadie by entertaining such overtures.

He took a step back. "Richmond is a fine city. And I'm certain that, should you visit, you would have much to occupy your time. So much, I doubt you would have time for visiting a *friend*."

She frowned. That was certainly not what she had expected, and it showed.

The thundering of hoofbeats filled the area. And, soon enough, the stage appeared around the far corner of the small stretch.

"That will be your ticket out of this place." She sighed and moved nearer where he stood once more. "Farewell, Mr. Anderson. I do hope to see you again." The woman set a hand to his arm and leaned closer than she needed to.

He pulled his arm back as gently as possible and took a step back and toward his aunt. "Ah...I thank you for your kindness. Good day, Miss Higgins."

She made a small sound that seemed more than a little put out before she turned and sauntered off.

As David watched the stage unload, knowing the time for his departure was forthcoming, he again questioned his decision. Sadie may need him regardless of what she had said. But was that his responsibility? Was that wise?

As he considered their last interaction, her words sliced into his heart once more. No, this was best. For all involved.

CHAPTER 17
Weary

"Miss Sadie," a voice called, accompanying the knocking on the door.

Sadie stirred to life. Slowly.

How long had she slept? It felt as if she'd just lain down a few minutes ago. The nights were long, watching Mother. But she could not ask any of the others to do so. Mrs. Wallem and Aunt Jane had been wonderful to be vigilant over Mother during the day. Covering the night hours was the least Sadie could do.

"Miss Sadie, may I come in?" the voice became more insistent.

Sadie struggled to sit up. "Yes. Please do."

The door opened and Mrs. Wallem slipped in. "There is someone here to see you."

Sadie groaned and fell back on the bed. "Send them away."

Mrs. Wallem moved toward the bed. "Pardon, I would have done so, but it is Mrs. Amanda Miller. I wasn't certain you would have me turn her aside."

Amanda? What business did she have?

As much as Sadie wanted to continue to sleep, she couldn't refuse Mrs. Miller. The woman had been kind and helpful. There was little reason to lose friends over a bit of sleep. As it was, Sadie had precious few she could rely on. That number having just shrunk a few days ago.

The tightness in Sadie's chest returned. Why did she have to think on David? She'd best put him out of mind and out of her heart. If she knew what was best, she would.

"Help me into something more presentable," she said as she sat up and swung her feet over the edge of the bed.

Mrs. Wallem's gaze softened.

Sadie looked away. She couldn't stand the pity anymore. Yes, she appreciated the woman's concern, but this was too much for Sadie's worn nerves.

"I'd prefer the blue and yellow dress. If it is pressed."

"Of course," Mrs. Wallem said as she stepped to the wardrobe. "I believe it was pressed a few days ago."

How Mrs. Wallem kept up with the household things while tending Mother was beyond Sadie. If only there was more help. Not that she'd dare ask Alice for assistance. There was little more than spite and neediness from her cousin.

Though there was no reason to rush, Sadie did encourage more speed out of Mrs. Wallem. She did not wish to keep Amanda waiting longer than necessary. After Mrs. Wallem buttoned up the back of the dress, Sadie pulled her hair up and pinned it. Not the most pulled together she'd ever been. But these last couple of days had seen worse, too.

In a matter of moments, Sadie descended the stairs and strode to the parlor. How was she to do this? She paused just short of the large receiving room. Perhaps she should have insisted Mrs. Wallem dismiss the rancher's wife. But she didn't have it in her to ask such. Though, she wasn't certain she had an hour of entertaining in her either. What could the woman within want?

Drawing in a steadying breath, Sadie stepped forward and into the parlor.

Amanda Miller had seated herself on Sadie's favorite settee. She stood as Sadie entered.

"Please, don't worry with that." Sadie managed a smile. "Make yourself comfortable."

Sadie moved farther into the space and took a seat opposite. But that only gave her a full on view of the chair that David would always take, beside the settee.

"Is something the matter?" Amanda said after a moment of silence.

Sadie realized she stared at the vacant seat and brought her attention back to her guest. "No. It's nothing."

Amanda did not seem satisfied by Sadie's words.

"What can I do for you?" It occurred to Sadie that her last interaction with Amanda had been a few days ago at the Miller Ranch. When she and David had...been close. Was Amanda here to talk about David? Sadie prayed not. She wouldn't be able to keep her raw emotions in check.

Amanda fidgeted with the handle of a basket beside her. Where had that come from? Had it been here the whole time? Sadie really must be tired and her mental faculties compromised.

"I only wanted to make a social call. And Cook wanted me to bring you some fresh bread."

"Oh. That is thoughtful of Cook. We appreciate that very much."

Amanda watched her.

"As I also appreciate the time you took to come by." Sadie could kick herself for neglecting her manners.

But Amanda only watched with the gentlest smile. "How is your mother?"

What did the woman know—if anything? Sadie couldn't be certain. Yet there was no reason she could think of to hide the reality from her friend. "She is...well. But requires more attention than before. She injured herself on the stairs a few days ago."

"Oh? That is too bad. I'm sorry to hear that."

Sadie believed her. These were not just platitudes. Though Sadie could do nothing but shrug.

"How will you manage everything?"

What was behind that question? There was no hint of accusation, yet Sadie searched for it. She just couldn't seem to accept the concern. Not after everything that had happened. It would be best if Sadie satisfied herself that she could not lean on anyone—save perhaps Mrs.

Wallem. Though Sadie couldn't stop herself from wondering if Mrs. Wallem, too, would abandon them.

"I will do what I can." Sadie kept her response short as emotion welled in her throat. Why wouldn't Amanda say anything about David? Part of Sadie wanted very much to hear about him. And part of her couldn't bear to sit and let Amanda speak on the matter.

"Sadie..." Amanda's words soothed. "You are ragged from worry and pushing yourself."

Sadie looked to the side. Did she present so terribly? Did she care?

"You cannot keep this up." Amanda's indictment was not harsh, but it pushed something painful into Sadie's gut. And she found herself biting her lip to keep herself in check.

"How is...that is...I wondered if..." Sadie couldn't bring herself to ask. Even as she couldn't stop herself from broaching the subject.

"David left on the stage earlier today." The words were kind but spoken with finality.

Sadie licked her lips and looked down at her hands. She wanted to say something but could only nod.

Amanda stood and moved to the chair beside Sadie's. She set a hand on Sadie's forearm. "You aren't alone in this."

Sadie's throat ached with her effort to contain her grief. And her shoulders shook. The tears were coming. A torrent took hold of her.

She shifted to look at Amanda, no longer able to stop the tears making trails down her face. Could the woman truly mean to come alongside her? Dare Sadie risk trusting someone else?

"I know you have been through much. But my family are good people, ready to aid in any way they can. That includes those close to me —Cook and Owen, Cutie and Mariena, Dan and Lily, Slim and Ada..."

"Why?" Sadie's eyes now burned. "Why would you care?"

"Because I was you. But for the grace of God and the love of a good man, I would be destitute."

Sadie could no longer hold her gaze, so she looked at her lap again.

"And because...you are now a part of that family."

Sadie jerked her head up once more, but Amanda's visage was now blurry.

"A family that sticks together—no matter what."

Setting her face in her hands, Sadie let loose her cries. At some point, Amanda wrapped an arm around her and pulled her closer. Was this what it was to have friends? To have support? To experience mercy? It overwhelmed her tattered heart.

David settled into a chair at the only available table in the restaurant. Finally, a larger dining space and hope of a meal that would be more on-par with what he was used to. Not that it was a certainty. For Tucson was still a rather wild place. But it was bigger than Wharton City—much bigger. And that gave him reason to hope.

He hadn't had a well pulled together meal since...since he dined with Sadie at her home. That thought brought a pang of regret. Mulling over that for a moment, he shoved the memories to the side. What he was doing was for the best. For both of them.

The server came by and greeted him and Aunt Sylvia.

While Aunt Sylvia asked after the specials, he considered his options. There were quite a few—including things that he had not enjoyed in the last couple of months. And surprisingly fine dishes for such a place. Should he have the roast goose? That had not been available to him in Wharton City.

The server shifted her focus to him. "What about you, sir?"

"The chicken and dumplings look good."

Aunt Sylvia cocked her head. Was his request so strange? For certain, it had taken him by surprise.

"They are, sir. Very fine choice."

He nodded and handed his menu back.

"I did not expect you would choose something so provincial. Didn't we have that only a few days ago?" Her curiosity was fitting, he had to admit. The chance to have something more elegant had presented itself, and he chose chicken and dumplings—a meal he'd had numerous times these last months.

Then why had he?

"Ah yes," Aunt Sylvia said as she looked past him in thought. "We had that when Miss Perkins came to the ranch."

That couldn't be it. Had he been drawn to the dish because it reminded him of the last pleasant encounter with Sadie? He frowned.

"Something amiss?" Aunt Sylvia took a sip of her water. Why must she pry so?

He shook his head. "Nothing. Just thinking."

"I see." A smile graced her features. "About Miss Perkins?"

So bold. Everyone had become too bold with him of late. "I am only...thinking about that meal. Cook certainly has a way about the kitchen."

Aunt Sylvia nodded, but her grin did not fall in the least. What could he do if she wished to think more of his order than she ought?

Without further response from him, Aunt Sylvia did not speak more. She maneuvered the silver on the table and glanced out the window at the busy street beyond.

What did it matter what she thought anyway?

He rubbed a hand on the linen table covering and looked about the dining area. It was crowded, almost uncomfortably so. Though, that boded well for his coming entree. Didn't the hordes of people signal that the food was good?

A couple of patrons from a table nearby left. David tried not to worry himself with the cleaning and reseating. But he had nothing to busy his mind except the intrusive memories. And he did not wish to give credence to those.

Two men took the empty seats. Was that...Mr. Collins? David looked away, not wanting the man to recognize him. What was the new bank manager from Wharton City doing here? It was odd, to say the least.

"David, be a dear and—"

He held up a finger to halt Aunt Sylvia's statement.

She glared at him, an eyebrow arched.

Leaning forward, he urged her to do so as well. "The bank manager from Wharton City is at that table," he said in a harsh whisper.

Her eyes widened. Had Brandon or Amanda confided in her about the things that had happened to Sadie? It seemed likely. She maneuvered to the side to look over David's shoulder.

"No," he hissed. "Don't look."

She jerked upright and nodded. Then she peered down at her table setting as if trying to be discreet.

David focused again on what was being said behind him.

"I need to...confiscate a property. For the good of the town," Mr. Collins said.

"Yes?" the other man's deeper baritone almost seemed bored.

"It would be good if the judge could see things my way." Mr. Collins lowered his voice. The words were difficult to discern.

"You speak as though I have undue influence over such things." The man became defensive but softened his tone as well.

"Not at all." Mr. Collins' voice tripped as if nervous. "I only mean that it would help all involved if the judge were apprised of the situation beforehand. Knew the right places to look."

"I see."

Who was this man to the judge? A clerk? A law man? Who could have such influence over the judge?

"It is probably no matter. The lawyer that was a thorn in my side will be leaving Wharton City, if he hasn't already. Miss Perkins will be on her own. And she has more bark than bite."

"And you are certain her legal aid has abandoned her?"

Is that what David did? Abandon Sadie? Was there any other way to see it?

"Completely. I secured the information from a very reliable source." Mr. Collins' voice held more confidence.

"Might I ask who?"

David resisted the urge to lean back in their direction. He didn't want to chance being recognized.

"Between the sheriff and deputies, I have a good handle on the situation even if her mouthy cousin wasn't flitting about. But that woman confirmed my information."

Sadie's cousin was feeding the other side information? Intentionally? She didn't seem to have the highest regard for Sadie. Though she also seemed rather dim...enough to give away important information?

He could blame Miss Alice Higgins all he wanted, but the truth was, Sadie was in trouble. The situation became grim. She might very well lose everything. And there was no one of means looking out for her.

The two men moved on to rather mundane discussion and David delved deeper into his own thoughts. If he hadn't left, Sadie's chances would be better. But his father had summoned him. That was no small thing. What would happen to his partnership, his career if he defied the man?

"Aunt Sylvia," David said, looking up at her.

"Yes?" she kept her voice low as if they conspired.

"We have to catch the next stage. We're going back to Wharton City."

CHAPTER 18

Rethinking

L oud knocking on the door disrupted Sadie's tentative concentration. She shook her head. Having just retired to her room after a long night sitting up with Mother, she didn't need this.

The knocking continued.

Who was there? And would someone answer it?

"Agh," she grunted as she sat up. Then she rushed from her room and down the stairs.

She passed Alice in the hall. What was wrong with her that she couldn't get the door? It was a fleeting thought, however. There wasn't much hope that Alice would do anything helpful.

"You're going to receive like that?" she muttered.

Sadie didn't offer her so much as a cursory glance. She knew what Alice referred to. Her clothes were likely in a state. No different than how she had been these last several days. No one in the town saved much kind thought for her, so why continue to care?

Alice moved to continue toward the stairs.

Sadie paused and turned toward her retreating cousin. "Why do you despise me so?"

Alice whirled. "Whatever do you mean?" There was a coldness to her tone.

"It seems you take pleasure in my hardship. You have never spoken two kind words to me in all the time we have been acquainted. And I wonder why that is. What did I ever do to bring out such animosity from you?"

Alice's lips curled and then settled. But she didn't speak.

Sadie shrugged and turned back toward the door. There was little hope she'd actually get an answer.

"Yes." Alice shot out. "It is true. There is no love spent here."

Sadie spun. Would Alice truly spill it all right here, right now?

Alice stepped closer. "You have always had everything. Everything. Money, privilege, a father who doted on your every word."

Sadie widened her gaze. Why these words should surprise her she didn't know.

Alice pushed out a breath. "And now the tables have turned. Yet, my mother is willing to drop everything to come and help *you*. It must be nice for everyone to fawn over you so."

Another knock sounded on the door as well as a muffled entreaty.

"You'd best see who it is," Alice said as she turned. "Likely someone else coming to move heaven and earth for you."

Sadie opened her mouth but could not form words as her cousin walked off.

The knocks on the door became louder. She needed to attend to it.

Sadie picked up step and, as she closed in on the front door, Mrs. Wallem stepped out from the dining room. "Oh, Miss Sadie! I apologize that disturbed you. I was quite—"

She waved the woman off. "Do not worry yourself. I am awake and able to receive."

Sadie had a thought that it could be Amanda Miller. The woman had said she would check in on Sadie with some frequency. Amanda had such a tender heart for Sadie's situation. It nearly brought tears to Sadie's eyes just thinking about it.

Reaching for the latch, Sadie nodded to Mrs. Wallem, who turned back toward the dining area. But as Sadie opened the door, she wished for Mrs. Wallem's presence.

Deputy Travers stood on the front porch. With a sly grin on his face. His features fell as he took her in.

"Miss Perkins, I didn't expect to find you...so out of sorts."

Sadie didn't have time for this. She pushed out a breath. "What do you want?"

He set a hand against the doorframe, leaning to that side and closer to Sadie. "Does an eligible man need a reason to call on an unattached young woman?" Whatever he was doing with his face in that moment—something akin to a scrunch and a wink—did nothing to enhance his appearance.

"This lady needs a reason," Sadie countered, stepping opposite.

"Well then," he straightened and set his hands to his belt. The way his revolver shifted as he did so, she couldn't miss it. "I'm here to continue our conversation."

Sadie wanted to feign confusion, but that would only prolong this encounter. Still, she couldn't conjure a response.

"Have you," he said as he tilted his head forward, "thought about what I said?"

"Actually, I have." She crossed her arms.

His eyebrows arched. "And?"

"No." She firmed her jaw muscles.

"No?" His crooked smile fell. And his gaze hardened. "You can't mean that."

"I promise you I do." She took a step back, moving to close the door.

He stuck out a hand, halting the door's momentum. "I don't think you understand the situation."

She swallowed, resisting the urge to bite at her lip.

"I am your only hope here, darling. Your last hope to save this..." He waved a hand as if he could encompass the whole of the property. "...place."

Sadie pulled in a long breath. She would not let him get a rise out of her. "I will take my chances."

His mouth widened and he shook as if laughing. "That you certainly can."

Why was he so amused?

"And sooner than you think." He narrowed his gaze. "The judge arrives tomorrow."

Tomorrow? How was she not privy to this information? Without time to prepare, without David's help...was there any reason for her to think she might succeed? Then she looked at Deputy's Travers' sardonic grin. Yes. She would have to.

"I appreciate you making the trip to tell me."

His eyes widened. The laughing stopped.

"If that is all, I have things to attend to." She lifted her chin and set her features.

The shock on his face gave her some measure of satisfaction.

She pressed on the door once more.

He did not loosen his grip on the wood and, additionally, put forth a foot to prevent any further movement. "I'm warning you, Miss Perkins. This won't go well for you if you insist on taking it farther."

"And I said, 'good day' to you." Her heart beat harder as she tried to stare him down. What could she do if he refused to go? Or worse... decided to aggress upon her? Would he?

The sound of a horse and wagon wheels rumbled. Drawing closer.

Deputy Travers turned in the direction of the path.

Who set upon this property? Was it friend or foe?

Travers shot a look at her.

She did her best to hold her head up as if she expected whoever neared.

The cart came into view—it was Amanda and another woman.

Deputy Travers sneered and backed away. "This isn't over."

Sadie minded her breathing, doing what she could to keep it from betraying her nervousness. But her pulse settled as the deputy continued to walk toward his horse. She watched as he untied the reins and mounted.

Amanda was near enough to have seen the man by now, but he didn't wait or acknowledge them, just took off in the opposite direction. Where was he headed? That wasn't the way to town.

Yet she didn't concern herself with the deputy or his intentions one moment more. Even if she did push his words and the truth of them to the side. That was a problem for another day.

David wanted to move closer to the window. Were they near Wharton City? Surely, they had been traveling long enough. But he had only to glimpse the dust cloud surrounding the stage to think better of it.

"You seem rather anxious," Aunt Sylvia said, watching David's hands.

They were warm as he had been rubbing them together. Indeed, he could not deny that he was nervous about their arrival. How would Sadie receive him? When last they spoke, she had dismissed him rather adamantly.

Would he let her put him aside again? Not knowing what he did about the mounting forces against her. If the judge had been misinformed, or worse—bribed—she would need all the help she could get.

And he refused to abandon her again.

The tempo of the hoofbeats altered. And, keeping his distance, David looked out the window in time to see the first structure heralding the coming town. It gave way to more. They had made it!

He turned to his aunt. What was he to do with her? It was not likely he could—or should—delay in getting to Sadie. Perhaps he might secure a horse in town. But how to get Aunt Sylvia back to the ranch?

She had insisted he leave her in Tucson. That was out of the question. Though she could probably fend for herself, he had been entrusted with her care. He would not fail her.

But could he wait until she was safely with the Millers? It had been difficult enough to pause for the night in Tucson, awaiting the next coach to Wharton City. This was impossible.

The horses slowed, and the stage came to a stop just beyond the telegraph office. It was all David could do to wait for someone to open the door.

He practically leapt from within. And so quickly, the driver had little time to stumble back.

"Pardon me," David offered. Then he spun to help Aunt Sylvia out, his pulse racing faster than he'd ever remembered.

The driver grunted and moved off toward the bags, which were being unloaded.

"Aunt Sylvia," David's words rushed out almost as quickly as his breathing. "I—"

She held up a hand. "Go to her. I will be fine at the café until arrangements can be made."

He nodded, his chest expanding at her understanding and the realization he would see Sadie within the hour.

After ensuring Aunt Sylvia was set for the café, David crossed the street to the small livery. It took some time for the stable hand to saddle a horse to rent him. And every second that eked by only intensified his tension. After several long minutes, the man and horse appeared.

David thanked the man and pulled himself atop the mare. Then he was off.

The ride to the Perkins' home always seemed to drag. Never more so than today. Even as he pushed the horse, he couldn't speed the dragging time.

At last, the stately home became visible on the horizon. And as he neared, he could see a familiar wagon just outside the main entrance. Who had come from the Miller Ranch? Maybe it was a godsend. Perhaps whoever was here might collect Aunt Sylvia on their way back to the ranch. He had little time to consider that before he halted his horse, dropped down, and tied off the reins.

Then he knocked. He took a minute to wipe his forehead. The whole of him perspired. From the exertion of the ride? Or his own nerves?

Mrs. Wallem opened the door.

"Mr. Anderson?" She was clearly shocked to see him.

He offered her a nod. "Yes, I need to speak with Miss Perkins."

Mrs. Wallem didn't seem so sure, but she stepped back and opened the door a bit wider. "This way. She's resting, but I will ask if she would like to speak with you."

He grimaced, hating to disturb Sadie's rest, and fearing that she would outright refuse him before he had a chance to plead his case. What if he didn't even get to see her?

Mrs. Wallem closed the door and held up an arm in the direction of the parlor.

He stepped toward the hall, trying to manage his emotions.

"David?" The voice came from the stairway.

He turned.

And there she was. Sadie stood at the top of the stairs, eyes wide and features unreadable.

He found himself unable to speak. Or even breathe.

Sadie slid a hand along the rail and descended. She was coming toward him.

It occurred to him that she had not outright dismissed him. But that was far from an open welcome. What would it be?

As she neared, everything else in his awareness dropped away. It was only her. He swallowed, taking her in. The memory of their kiss flitted into his mind unhindered. Dare he dwell on it? It may be best to push that out of mind.

She reached the landing and stepped closer.

How had he remained glued to the spot? He neither advanced nor spoke.

"I..." She cleared her throat. "I thought you had left." Her voice shook a bit.

"I did. But I couldn't." He found his own voice catching. "I couldn't stay away."

She gazed into his eyes. There was no ire there, only that vulnerability...seeking him.

He closed the distance. And though he wanted to envelop her in his arms, he resisted. It might be unwelcome. Besides, Mrs. Wallem stood an arm's length away. So, he lifted a hand toward Sadie, hoping against hope that she would slide hers into it. Would all be well then?

She paused, as did the world in that moment.

He sucked in a breath for lack of air.

Then she leaned in and fell against his chest.

He didn't care who was watching; he held her. Tightly.

"I'm sorry," she choked out. "So sorry."

David rubbed her back and ran a hand down her hair. "I know. I am, too."

A warmth spread through him, reaching to every limb, every part of him. And he felt whole again.

CHAPTER 19
Danger

S adie reluctantly pulled back from David. It was difficult to make herself do so. His concern and care were evident in the way he'd held her. And she relished it, wanted to revel in it a bit longer.

But Mrs. Wallem was likely becoming uncomfortable. Sadie looked to where the woman was.

Or had been.

Where had Mrs. Wallem gone?

Sadie was embarrassed that their display had given Mrs. Wallem cause to sneak off. But she could not pretend she wasn't grateful for the woman's sensitivity. Sadie had needed to be near David.

"Are you all right?" His voice was tender even as it probed.

"Yes...no." She shook her head as she peered up at him. "There is much to tell."

He nodded. "Shall we continue on to the parlor then?" As he turned, he startled. "Wasn't Mrs. Wallem just here?"

"Yes." Sadie's face warmed. "I think she slipped off to allow us some measure of privacy.

"Ah, I see." David's words were laced with his smile.

She tried to shake off her nerves but could not. His nearness did something to her. Something not at all unpleasant.

"Shall we?" he repeated as he indicated the hall toward the parlor.

She nodded and strode toward the receiving space.

"I noticed a wagon outside. Do you have visitors?" David's words were tentative. As if he hated to pry.

"Oh, Amanda Miller and a Mariena Reynolds. Someone you know?"

He had heard the name. Was that the woman who married one of the former ranch hands? The couple working to set up a school for the native children in the area? There was no way David could keep up with it all. "I do not."

"These wonderful women have come to help around the house. Amanda insisted. They are cleaning and cooking. Such a blessing."

"It is a good thing they are here. Aunt Sylvia remained in town. Perhaps they can collect her from town."

Sadie nodded.

They moved within the parlor, and Sadie took her seat on the settee and watched as David settled into the chair beside her.

Silence thickened the air between them. She didn't know what to say or where to start.

Thankfully, David broke the tension. "I wasn't certain that you would welcome me."

Why did he have to address that so quickly? Her nervousness grew, bringing a tightness between her shoulder blades. Where would he go with this?

"Sadie," he said as he took her hand in his. "I am truly sorry for what happened...and how it happened. It was never my intention to hurt you. Or abandon you."

She looked into his eyes. "I know. There is enough blame for both of us to share. I certainly behaved terribly."

He squeezed her hand. "No more than my actions called for."

She set her other hand over their clasped fingers. "Let's agree to not speak of it again then."

He nodded and licked his lips. Was he about to speak? Silence filled in the space separating them.

"I had a visitor." She drew in a breath to continue, but he spoke before she could.

"Who?" His eyebrows gathered. Had her tone given away that this was an unwelcome guest?

She swallowed. "Deputy Travers."

His hands tensed, tightening on hers. And David seethed, "What did he do?"

She appreciated his concern, but she didn't want to give the deputy's visit more weight than it merited. "Nothing. He came to announce that the judge will be here tomorrow."

His eyes widened just a bit. Then they narrowed. "Is that all?"

As if that weren't enough. She bit at her lip, wanting, and not wanting to share more.

"Sadie, what else did he say?" David's eyes became more serious. His anger was a breath away.

She couldn't—and didn't want to—avoid the issue. He should know, shouldn't he? "The deputy reminded me of our earlier chat and asked if I had reconsidered."

David's mouth became a thin line. "It bothered you."

She nodded. "He made an empty threat as he left."

"Oh?" One of David's eyebrows arched, and his lips became even smaller as if the muscles around them tightened. Was he becoming so coiled?

"Well, he tried to threaten me. I am not worried," she lied. The truth was she didn't know what the deputy was capable of or what lengths he would go to. But David was here now. Surely that limited Travers' ability to visit harm upon her by abusing the law.

"What did he say?" David's shoulders stiffened.

"He said, 'This isn't over.'" She rubbed at his hand with her thumb. "But he was angry. I'm certain he didn't mean it."

David pushed out a breath. "We have to report this."

"To whom? Sheriff McAllen? Why would he believe us? Please," she said as she leaned in a bit, "let's not make this worse."

He watched her for a moment before nodding. But his spine did not ease in the least.

Should she delay the rest of the conversation? The things she needed to know? But she couldn't. "Why did you come back?"

His gaze met hers, and his eyes softened. "I realized how wrong I was. That I was abandoning you."

That wasn't all either. He was holding something back as well. "And?"

He searched her eyes. What was he looking for? At length, he let out another breath and said, "I came across Mr. Collins in Tucson."

"Mr. Collins? What was he doing there?" Now it was her turn to be perplexed and a bit upset. Did David truly come back for her sake alone? Or was there something more to it? Perhaps she wasn't enough after all.

"He—" Then David looked off toward the door. "Do you smell that?"

She sniffed. There was a smoky scent in the air. "Maybe someone burned dinner."

David cocked his head to the side and seemed to weigh the situation.

Then a scream shattered any hint of peace that remained.

Mother!

Sadie shot to her feet and David alongside her.

She tried to move forward around him, but he pressed her behind himself.

"Something is wrong. That was my mother," Sadie struggled to breathe. Had someone hurt Mother? Was Mother in some sort of trouble?

David moved toward the door. Sadie stayed close behind him.

They stepped out into the hall, and the smell nearly knocked Sadie over.

David covered the lower portion of his face with his sleeve. "Don't breathe it in."

What was he saying? It was that cantankerous oven! Still, she obeyed, copying his movements.

Another scream shot through the hall.

David moved in that direction.

Only a couple of paces into the hall, Sadie became aware of a sweltering heat. What was happening? The sensation became more intense as they neared the back of the house.

David reached for the latch on Mother's bedroom door, then jerked it open.

Smoke poured out of the room. The house was on fire!

David jerked back from the onslaught of smoke and coughed. He tried to keep his mouth and nose covered, but it was difficult. Questions flew through his mind: What had happened here? How did the fire get started? Where was Sadie's mother? How was he to keep Sadie safe?

Sadie rushed forward. "Mother!"

He held her back. "You can't go rushing in like that."

"But my mother!" Sadie's eyes widened, and her voice became frantic.

"I will get your mother out. You make sure everyone gets to safety. Let's hope no one else was back here." He hunched over and prepared to enter the room.

Sadie didn't move, just stared into the room.

"Go," he commanded. "I will get her out. I promise."

She finally nodded, eyes watering, and turned opposite.

Relief rushed through David. At least Sadie was away from immediate danger. He shifted his focus back to the smoke-filled bedroom.

"Mrs. Perkins?" he called as he entered.

Her screams had become moans and whimpers.

The room was dark but for the flash of flames and what light he could see streaming through the window. Where could she be?

He stumbled farther into the room. And though he wasn't much for prayer, he shot out a simple plea. *God, please help me find her.*

David had only been in this room the one time. He took a moment to conjure an image from memory.

The bed was to the right and against the wall. As he recalled, a wardrobe cabinet sat across the room directly in front of him. And a chair had been situated to the left.

He continued into the room, careful to not trip over anything—heaven forbid he step on Mrs. Perkins. But he homed in on the sounds she made, though they became quieter.

There. To the right and on the floor. A heap. It could be Sadie's mother.

David bent over it. Indeed, as he put his free hand to the lump, it gave way under his touch and groaned.

"Mrs. Perkins?" he tried again.

No acknowledgement from her. Had she taken in too much smoke? Or had she been burned?

He wasn't certain, but it was clear that she needed to get out of here. Soon. So, he removed his hand from his own face and, shifting her to her back, lifted her. David had never been a very physical person, but he was pleased to note that she was not heavy.

Pressing back toward the opening to the room, he maneuvered to the front door and out into the yard.

"Thank the Lord!" Mrs. Wallem helped him lower Mrs. Perkins to the ground as Mrs. Higgins fussed over her.

He glanced around. Alice was nearby, but where was Sadie? Amanda? Mariena? Then he looked to Mrs. Wallem. "Where—?"

"Sadie insisted they try to put the fire out." The woman seemed apologetic. As well she should be. How could she let those women attempt something so dangerous?

He spun and ran to the back of the house. Sure enough, there they were, having formed a line from the water pump to the outside of Mrs. Perkins' bedroom as best he could tell. That portion of the house had suffered. And he wondered...was the fire set out here? Or from within the bedroom? There wasn't time to spend on speculation. They had to douse the flames if they could. Unless they should consider the whole house a loss.

The ladies made progress, but it was slow. They had to get it out quickly. Rushing inside, he grabbed the first blanket he could find and carried it back out to the water pump. Soaking it as much as possible in the few moments he allowed himself, he moved to the structure and slapped at the fire.

Their work seemed to take hours, but at length, they began to see progress. But how bad was it within the room?

He gripped the wet blanket and ran into the bedroom once more.

The fire did not rage as it had before; they had isolated it. He again used the cloth to stamp out the fire that remained and continued several minutes after the last spark disappeared.

Hands pulled at his arm.

He turned.

Sadie stared up at him, her hair mussed, her face covered in black streaks. "It's over."

He sucked in a breath and let it out then nodded.

She surveyed the damage, becoming eerily quiet as she did so. What must be going through her mind?

Though he wanted space to continue drawing in air, he stepped to her and wrapped an arm around her shoulders.

She remained as she was, unresponsive to his touch.

Still, he held on to her.

She rubbed at her cheeks. Because she was crying?

Yes, this was devastating. And more so with everything she had already endured. How much more would the woman have to live through?

But they were all alive and well, if not a little worse for wear.

"How is Mother?" she whispered.

"Mrs. Wallem is with her."

Sadie nodded as she dropped her head.

He turned and lifted her chin with a finger. "Hey. We're all right. That's what matters."

She sniffled and wiped at the tears that continued to fall. "Yes. We are."

Yet he would wager not all were of grief. Some must be relief.

He, too, scanned the room, uncertain what he was looking for. The back wall was badly damaged, and the contents of the room were beyond salvaging. But these were only things, he reminded himself. What would he have done if Sadie had been injured or...lost in the fire? If he hadn't been here and the fire had gotten out of control and she tried to rescue her mother? Though it was only a thought, his chest ached. He couldn't lose her. Not now. Not after he reconciled how he cared for her.

Something caught his attention. A lantern lay on the floor, smashed.

Had Sadie's mother tried to light the lantern? For what reason? It was daytime. Perhaps she had dropped the piece and started the fire. The way this room had been charred so much more so than the rest of the back of the house, it could make sense.

But dare he share his suspicion with Sadie?

He wrapped his other arm around her, drawing her more into himself and holding her. Right now, all that mattered was that she was well. Everything else could take its place at another time.

CHAPTER 20

Concerned

S adie looked across the back of the house. It was strange how the fire had been isolated to one side. Perhaps because of how quickly they acted in putting it out. She wiped her hands against an already dirty skirt and moved more of Mother's clothing to the pile. They would try to launder these things, but the chance of saving them was not great.

David directed Mr. Miller and one of the ranch hands with the sections of the wall they removed.

Sadie was once again overwhelmed at the kindness of these people, who had come to her aid. Especially David. What would have happened had he not been here? And then he had insisted on staying the night. It was true that his presence in the house had made her safer. What if the culprit had decided to come back? To finish what he started or do worse?

She grimaced. But anger would do her no good in this moment.

Amanda reached for the next garment and continued scrubbing as Mariena hung the finished things on the clothesline.

What would Sadie do without this support? She took in a deep breath. Indeed, she was not friendless as once suspected.

"You all right?" Amanda asked as she dunked Mother's purple dress into the vat of soapy water.

"I am." Sadie met her gaze. "Just thinking."

Amanda nodded. "I'm sure you are."

"I don't know what to do from here." The words were out before Sadie could stop them.

"Perhaps you should take a rest for a few minutes." Amanda arched a brow. "This has to have been overwhelming for you."

Sadie nodded but didn't move from where she surveyed the work being done.

David turned. Did he sense she stared at his back?

Her face warmed and she offered him a small smile. Things were still too new with them for her to feel free to just glare at him like she was.

His mouth widened in a grin, but his eyes remained serious. What was behind that? Worry? For her? The home? Or their pending appearance before the judge? As if she could narrow her own concerns to just one.

He strolled toward her.

She had not meant to pull him from his work. But she hadn't the heart to turn him away either.

"You should sit down. You look exhausted." His voice was tender, yet firm.

"No more so than you." She wished she could have offered him the guest room, but it sat above Mother's former bedchambers and had been damaged as well. So, he had settled in the parlor for the evening on a pallet. That had chipped away at her throughout the sleepless night.

"I'm well enough," he said as he touched her arm. "It's you I'm worried about."

She looked to the ground. Everyone's kindness and attention weighed on her.

"Let's take a walk," he offered.

Meeting his gaze, she found his suggestion rather appealing. "Very well."

He shifted to lead her, but she halted him with a hand to his arm.

"But only for a little while. There is too much to do."

He did not seem to warm to that idea, but he nodded nonetheless. Then he stuck out an elbow in her direction.

She slid a hand into the crook there, and he led her away from the work, farther into the field beside the house.

The fresh air and bit of exercise did improve her constitution. This had been the better idea.

David brooded beside her. She could practically feel his anger coming off him. Certainly, the tightening of his muscles gave him away.

"What is it?" she asked, keeping her tone gentle.

He shook his head. Of course, she should expect no less. Much had happened. And he had proven that he cared for her. There was more to worry over than perhaps there was to be glad about.

"I...haven't heard whether or not the judge arrived as expected," she said, keeping her head down. Someone had to broach the subject.

"He did." David glanced at her for a second before setting his gaze toward the horizon.

"Oh?" She did wonder how he knew it. Hadn't he been here at the house since yesterday?

"Brandon told me."

Ah. Yes. Of course, his cousin would be keeping an ear to the ground in regards to these matters.

"And...unfortunately, they do not plan to delay anything on account of the fire."

She halted. "No?" Were these men completely heartless?

"The judge is expected in Tombstone in three days. There isn't any room to do so."

She frowned. "It's almost like someone planned the fire to make matters worse."

David watched her. Did he not agree? "We will be prepared."

"I only wish there was something I could do...some way to get justice for what he did." Her own ire settled in the pit of her stomach. Yes, this was all manipulated to make her situation unthinkably worse.

"He?" David's brow furrowed.

"Deputy Travers," Sadie pressed out. David's confusion confused her. "Who else?"

David's mouth seamed. Did he have nothing to say on the matter?

"Obviously, he made good on his threat. And rather timely, at that."

David looked out across the field toward the horizon. Why wasn't he responding? Did he not care after all?

"Can you imagine a worse possible time for this than right before we see the judge?"

"I cannot," he managed.

At least there was that. But something about his manner concerned her. It seemed as if he held something back. Dare she address it? Or let him tell her when he was ready?

"What can we do, after all? Sheriff McAllen will dismiss our accusation as if we were the aggressors." Then an idea hit her. "Perhaps the judge will listen. We can tell him that the deputy—"

"No." David's tone was firm. He looked at her again. His eyes were serious.

"What? Why ever not?"

David shifted and glanced away again. Then he settled his gaze on hers again. "Because I don't believe he set the fire."

She put a hand over her heart. "Who else would have done something like this? The townspeople are angry, sure, but *he* threatened me. *He* had a reason."

David did not pull his gaze away, but his eyes softened. "Sadie," he said as he took her hands, "the fire was started from inside the house."

What was he saying? Was he trying to communicate that someone snuck in? Or that one of her friends sabotaged her? She wouldn't hear it. "You can't think that Amanda or Mariena would—"

"No." His response was short.

She chewed at the inside of her lip. He certainly didn't think that Mrs. Wallem would... Or was he insinuating that Mother had done it? She tried to pull her hands free. "You can't be serious."

He held onto her fingers, not letting her slip away. "I'm sorry. But there was evidence of a shattered lantern in your mother's room. I saw it."

She felt sick. He couldn't mean that.

"I don't think it was a purposeful act. Perhaps your mother only meant to light the lantern."

Sadie shook her head. "We never leave her alone..." Her sentence fell as she realized that no one had been in the room with her. Unless they had abandoned her when the fire started. That seemed rather unlikely.

"I know it is not pleasant, but it's true." David looked into her eyes.

There was reason to see his concern for her there. But she didn't want to. She didn't want him to be right. Because if Mother, unsupervised, were capable of such, what did that mean?

David slid past the small crowd gathered on the planked sidewalk. It was the busiest time of day for the café. He hoped that Judge Smithers and Mr. Collins had secured a table already. Though, part of him wished to find one or the other alone. The reality was that Mr. Collins or his associate in Tucson had already had communication with the judge. But if it were up to him, the man would not spend outside time with either.

The people near David gave him a strange look. He didn't have to guess why. His suit, though clean from his trunk, had been in Sadie's house. The stench of smoke, though but a hint, was there.

He slipped within and spotted Mr. Collins laughing with the man he could only suppose was Judge Smithers. David frowned. This was not easing his worry in the least.

As he neared the table's empty chair, he nodded to the men. "Judge Smithers, I'm David Anderson, legal counsel for Mrs. Perkins."

The judge shook his hand. "Please, have a seat, Mr. Anderson."

Mr. Collins scowled. As if that would do anything to deter David.

The judge spoke as David sat. "Mr. Collins and I were just discussing a mutual friend in Chicago. Seems Mr. Collins has some rather...important friends."

"Or perhaps unfortunate friends." Mr. Collins winked at Judge Smithers.

That elicited another laugh from the judge. This was not going well. But David reminded himself that he had the law on his side. The judge may enjoy rubbing elbows with the banker, but that didn't mean he cared not for the letter of the law.

Judge Smithers waved over the server, and the men placed their orders. The others selected food, while David requested only coffee. He didn't have the stomach for Mr. Collins' grasping nature *and* food.

"Let's see if I have this correct, gentlemen." The judge settled his large hands on the table as he leaned forward. "I understand that there is a property in question."

"Yes," David said, preparing to make the most of this opportunity. "There is a clear—"

"Let's not get into all of that just yet," Judge Smithers said as he held up a hand. "We need not jump to the arguments just now. All in good time."

"Yes, Your Honor." David settled back into his chair. As much as he could.

"I want to be clear; I intend to settle this with as little to-do as possible. Let's keep this thing simple. After all, it is not a serious matter."

According to whom? David wondered. It was the Perkins' home. Their only hold on their livelihood. Their only chance to maintain their independence. Though there was much wisdom in not voicing his objections to the judge's statement.

"So, I would like to gather this afternoon to hear any testimony you want me to hear."

Mr. Collins nodded.

"I will make sure that Miss Perkins is there."

"Miss Perkins?" The judge seemed confused. "The property in question is owned by a single woman?"

"No, Your Honor," David said before Mr. Collins could pipe in. "I am referring to Miss Sadie Perkins, the daughter of Mrs. Eugenia Perkins. She will be testifying on her mother's behalf. She is familiar with all of the facts of the case."

"You are telling me that the woman who allegedly owns the property will not be appearing?" Judge Smithers did not look pleased.

"My clients do not think that is necessary. If you would hear what Miss Perkins has to say instead, I'm certain you would agree that—"

"I will hear from Mrs. Eugenia Perkins. Or I can decide this case right here and now."

A thickness filled David's chest and throat, but he attempted to keep his emotions in check. This was his forte. And he was good at what he did. Though he did feel a little backed into a corner. What exactly had the judge been told?

"Yes, Your Honor, I will see to it." David shot a look at Mr. Collins. The man offered a sly grin. Yes, there was more going on here than it seemed.

As if something was finally going David's way, the server showed up with his coffee and the judge's food. Another server followed with Mr. Collins' order.

"Now, then. That's settled." Judge Smithers picked up his fork. "Collins, did you say *Albert* Johnson?"

Conversation buzzed between the two men. David wasn't able to contribute much to the discussion, but he refused to leave the two alone.

Though he couldn't stop his mind from flitting to how he would address this new obstacle with Sadie. How were they to sidestep it? Then an idea came to him. Sadie wouldn't like it, but it just might save them from impending disaster.

CHAPTER 21
Trust

S adie scooped a bite of mashed potatoes into her mouth and smiled at Amanda's words. The Millers were quite the entertainment. How would Sadie get through this without them?

Alice scoffed and focused on her plate of food. She had not appreciated the Millers in the least. Which surprised Sadie. After all, if not for their help, the women would be work heavy and progress challenged.

Not that Alice would have helped.

They had accomplished much in these last twenty-four hours. It was almost unbelievable. They had saved several of Mother's dresses. And the back wall of the bedroom had been rebuilt. Then furniture from the guest room had replaced Mother's damaged pieces.

All in all, it eased Sadie's mind when Mother could move into the lone downstairs bedroom again. Safe from having to use the stairs.

With Mariena and Amanda helping to take shifts with Mother, it had lightened that burden as well. But David's words came back to her —hard words, but perhaps necessary. He had stressed again how difficult it was to keep everyone safe with Mother's mental decline and lack of control. The fire, if Mother did start it, had made a strong case. But where could Mother go and still be safe? Wasn't it best she remain home...with loved ones?

189

It was too much for Sadie to think about when there were so many other things happening. The least of which was the judge's arrival.

Even then she glanced at David across the table. He had returned just before dinner and begged off speaking with her until the meal had been finished. Though he was quiet. More so than usual. It unnerved Sadie.

As she watched, Mr. Miller leaned toward David and said something. Not that she could hear across the room and above the din of voices. Though she could monitor their reactions.

David frowned and said something back.

That brought a furrow to Mr. Miller's features, which only made her more anxious.

She glanced about the table settings; most everyone was finished. They had all settled into comfortable camaraderie. How was she to endure one minute more without knowing what David found out from his meeting with the judge?

Mrs. Wallem stood and began clearing plates. She appeared much more rested now that they'd had help. How could she ask the woman to go back to their harried, exhausting schedule of looking after Mother?

"It has been a pleasure," Aunt Jane said as she stood. "I have appreciated so much that you all have stepped in and helped my cousin and her sweet daughter."

This was rather odd. Was Aunt Jane preparing to make some kind of announcement? It left Sadie's nerves on edge.

"And I will be sad to go." Aunt Jane looked at Sadie. "But we must."

Sadie's stomach dropped. Had Alice brought this about? Was there no end to what her cousin would do to hurt her? How could Sadie do this without her aunt? Would her life always be two steps forward, one step back?

"Alice has expressed...and I agree...we have lingered for quite some time, and there are things at home which demand our attention."

Sadie chanced a glance toward Alice. Her smile was a little too wide. And when Alice set her gaze on Sadie, her eyes narrowed as well. It left a strange expression about her features—a not so pleasant one. Perhaps Aunt Jane was tired. Perhaps Alice had talked her into leaving. Perhaps

Aunt Jane needed peace…and rest. Whatever the reason for their departure, Sadie knew Alice had been involved.

Something passed between the cousins in that moment. While Sadie could hope that Alice would open her mind—and heart—she knew it wasn't likely. Yet rather than bad feelings toward her cousin, Sadie saw that Alice was in a sad state and had naught but compassion for her. Whatever Alice had said—or done—to convince Aunt Jane to go, Sadie would not hold it against her. At least one of them had to have a forgiving heart.

"I think I will retire for the evening. There is much to do in the next couple of days." Aunt Jane nodded and moved out into the hall.

Alice came alongside her mother and accompanied her toward the stairs.

Would Aunt Jane leave just after the trial then? What if things went badly for Sadie? Would Sadie have to beg shelter for herself and Mother with Aunt Jane? Or perhaps the Millers? That was almost unthinkable. That family had done so much already.

Sadie felt the intensity of someone's gaze on her. She turned and found David watching her. There was a sadness about his eyes. Did he pity her?

No, she told herself. He cared about her; that was what caused this sadness. It was unfortunate, this turn of events. And she was grateful for his…friendship? For whatever this was blossoming between them.

He tilted his head forward. Was he trying to indicate something?

It mattered little, she couldn't—and wouldn't—wait for him one moment more. She opened her mouth, but David broke into the silence first.

"Miss Perkins, might I offer you a turn about the property? I would very much like to see the progress made today," he said as he stood.

She nodded as she rose as well. "I would like that." She almost choked on the words. This anticipation was getting the better of her. Did she not trust David?

He came around the table and touched her elbow. "Shall we?"

She offered a smile she didn't feel and let him lead her from the room, down the hall, and out of the back of the house.

He grasped her fingers and led her hand to his arm. "It is looking rather nice." His gaze was on the wall.

"We finished laundering Mother's clothes, as well."

He nodded. "You've gotten a lot done today."

"It wasn't all me." Sadie looked at him. "I had great people helping me."

A smile pulled at his mouth but wouldn't take hold. Why did their encounters end up here—with him holding something back? She didn't know quite how to address it either.

"Would you like to see the progress in Mother's bedroom?" She stepped back toward the house.

He did not move, and his grip on her held her in place. "Not just yet. Might we take a stroll?"

She nodded. It was becoming apparent to her that either he thought best that way, or he preferred to have some level of privacy when delivering his news. Should she be worried?

He led her toward the field. Did he enjoy this prospect so well? It did provide a good view of the land beyond Mother's property. The gentle hills and tree dotted landscape.

They stopped and gazed at the horizon for a few moments. The sky turned colors—pinks, purples, oranges. Such a pleasant sight. It seemed as if the world cared not that Sadie faced so many obstacles. The sun continued its journey through the sky each day, and the moon did not fail to light the night. Just the same as it had always been.

"Sadie, there is no easy way to say what I must." David's words were soft. But they impacted Sadie as if he shouted them.

She didn't know whether to lean into his strength or pull away. So, she remained as she was.

"Judge Smithers is determined that your mother appear before him and testify."

The warmth drained from Sadie's features and her head swam.

"Sadie?" David's grip on her tightened as his arm surrounded her.

"Wh-what are we going to do? She can't very well...they'll find out about her sickness," she stammered. "And it will all be over."

He pressed her hand. "I have a plan."

She turned to look into his eyes. He seemed so confident, so hopeful.

"I think we should have Dr. Norwood testify to her mental state."

"But...he won't lie. He will tell them that she's not right and—" She pulled back.

He faced her and held her shoulders. "It's the only way, Sadie. You must see that your mother cannot remain here. And this will allow you to gain guardianship of her and her affairs. Then you can testify. The judge will have to accept your word in place of your mother's."

"No," Sadie shot out. "No, I won't do it."

"Listen to me...we are out of options."

"Then think harder! I won't betray my mother. On my life, I will not do that to her."

David pushed out a breath but kept his hold on her. "You have to face the reality of your mother's situation. I don't know how else to say this."

"Can't you...talk to the judge? You are a good lawyer. Surely, you can—"

"I can't. It won't work."

She furrowed her brow. "Won't work? How can you be sure if you don't try?"

He blew out the air in his lungs. As if he were relenting to something. "I overheard something...in Tucson."

She widened her eyes. "In Tucson?"

"Yes. Mr. Collins was there. He met with another man. Someone who Mr. Collins thought would have influence over the judge."

"Judge Smithers is corrupt?" How could this be?

"I'm not saying that. But there are those near him that are and may be whispering things in his ear. We must approach this offensively. It's the best thing for us—face it head on."

It was a lot of information to process. And it came quickly. David had come upon this meeting and come back? Because of that? Not solely because he cared? "Wait. You heard this in Tucson?"

"Yes," he said, pulling her a little closer. "In Tucson."

"And...you are just now telling me?" The pain she felt seeped into her words, and they accused.

"I wanted to tell you...tried to tell you. In the parlor, before the fire."

She couldn't fault him there. So much had happened that day. And in the two days since. "But...you said you came back because you didn't want to abandon me."

His eyes darkened.

"Is this really why? Because you felt I was outmatched?" The ache in her for his love became sharp. She hadn't realized how much she wanted —no, needed—him to just want to help her.

"I came back after hearing this, yes. It made me realize how much I care, Sadie. About what happens to you. About what happens to your mother and her property."

Her heart fell.

"But most of all," he said as he closed the gap that remained between them. "I came back because I love you."

Her pulse stuttered. What did he say? He loved her? She met his gaze again.

"Please, trust me. I know it's scary and it's a lot to ask. But I'm asking it." He tightened his arms to pull her closer, but she pressed hands to his chest to keep some distance. Then she lifted a hand to the side of his face, rubbing a thumb at the edge of his mouth.

She leaned forward and pressed her lips to his. The kiss was different than what they had shared. There was so much emotion in him...and it was as if he wanted to convey the whole of it through their exchange. His mouth moved over hers, deepening their contact, claiming her in a way she had not known.

When he did pull back, he rested his forehead on hers. "Will you trust me?" His words were husky.

"Yes." Her response surprised even her. But she knew this was right, what she and David had. And they had to stand together. Or else they would be torn apart.

David resisted the urge to pace. It would be best if he presented as confidently as possible. This was not going to be easy. But he would do it. For Sadie.

Everything inside him wanted to high tail it rather than risk failure. But he knew he was her only hope at this point. And he would not give in to his rathers. He would see this through.

He glanced about the church yard and wondered at Dr. Norwood's tardiness. Had the man been caught up with a patient? Lost track of time? That didn't seem likely—the whole of the town had apparently decided to show up for this trial. At least from the number of townsfolk going into the church, it seemed so.

David watched as the trickle of people became a steady flow. The time for him to go inside approached.

But where was Dr. Norwood? Or Sadie for that matter?

His gut clenched at the idea of going in unprepared. But he calmed it. This was his arena...the place where he felt most at ease. If only the risk to Sadie if he failed didn't overshadow him. That weighed heavily.

"Mr. Anderson," a breathless voice called from the direction of the main street.

David turned. Thank goodness...it was Dr. Norwood, his cheeks a little pink. Hopefully from exertion. Had he run the whole way here?

"Doctor," David said as he strolled to meet him.

"I apologize for my delay. There was an urgent matter at the clinic."

David held up a hand. "No need to explain. I'm just glad you are here."

"Do I have this right..." The doctor leaned toward David. "You want to me to testify to Mrs. Perkins addled mind?"

"Yes." David almost smiled at the man's surprise. With any luck, this strategy would throw the opposition a curve as well. "I only want you to tell the truth."

Dr. Norwood shrugged. "I can do that sure enough. If you think this is the best way to go about things."

"I do."

The clomping of hoofbeats nearby drew David's attention.

There, at the edge of the town, Sadie rode toward them. He couldn't be more relieved.

He stepped in that direction.

She didn't slow the horse until she was a few feet away. As she did so, he lifted his arms to assist her dismount. Sadie nearly fell against him as she hopped down.

"Is Dr. Norwood…" she started before she spotted him. "Good day, Doctor."

He moved to where she stood. "Good day, Miss Perkins. Are you in agreement with this plan?"

She looked at David, and for a moment his breath caught. That was his very question as well. Would she continue to follow his lead?

At length, she nodded. "I trust Mr. Anderson with my life."

That was quite the assertion. And he felt rather honored by it.

The area around them cleared as the hour for the trial drew near.

David looked to the doctor. "There are a couple of things I need to ask you."

"Anything," the doctor said as he nodded.

"If it isn't Miss Sadie Perkins and her lap dog," a man sneered from nearby.

David knew who it was before he turned.

Deputy Travers.

Hands clenched into fists, he spun toward the sound. "I would keep walking if I were you."

"And just what do you plan to do?"

Sadie grabbed for David's arm. "Don't," she said under her breath.

As much as he wanted to smash his fist into the man's face, he heeded her. There was no need to stoop to an uncivilized level—Travers' level.

"Just keep walking," David fairly growled.

"Ah, isn't that sweet. The lap dog knows some manners."

He would not be riled by this man. He refused to be.

"Why, Miss Sadie, I do believe I'd volunteer to be your next pupil any day," the deputy said as he passed, making a kissing sound in her direction.

Without thinking, David struck out, and his knuckles collided with Travers' nose.

The deputy grabbed for his face and shrieked. "I can't believe you hit me."

Sadie settled a hand around David's forearm.

"You won't get away with this." He turned to the doctor. "You saw him."

"Saw what?" Dr. Norwood offered a crooked smile.

The deputy stared openly as he alleviated his hold on his nose.

"I would keep pressure on that if I were you." Dr. Norwood narrowed his gaze as if examining the injury. "I'd be happy to patch you up. After I'm done here."

"After you're...what?"

"I think it's time," Sadie spoke up. "We don't want to keep the judge waiting."

Deputy Travers' jaw dropped. "You can't be serious."

Dr. Norwood patted him on the shoulder as they passed. "I'd keep the pressure on it and quit horsing around."

The three moved on toward the church, leaving the deputy and his intentions behind.

CHAPTER 22
Hope Lost

S adie wasn't quite prepared for the sight that greeted her. Stepping into the church, she was faced with a crowd. That fell silent. And stared.

Her face warmed and she halted under the scrutiny. Why had all these townsfolk come to see this? Were they so angry at her? Seeking some sort of justice for the wrongs her father committed? Maybe that was how it should be—her paying for the sins of her father. Though she felt as if she had suffered more than her fair share for simply being blood related to the man.

David's hand pressed the small of her back ever so gently. "Do not worry yourself with them. Truth will prevail."

She nodded numbly, taking what comfort she could from his presence, and took up step beside him.

The crowd parted as they passed, headed to the front of the building where an older man sat at a table on the dais. Was this the judge? He scowled as they neared. Was he so upset? With her? With this case?

David steered her to the right to a couple of chairs and small table waiting there.

Meanwhile, the townspeople came back to life, picking up conversations. The din of voices rose. But Sadie worked to shut them out.

The man she supposed to be the judge banged a gavel and ordered the people about to take a seat. A rush of movement surrounded her as they obeyed.

Then she faced the judge again.

"Mr. Anderson, this does not look like it could be Mrs. Eugenia Perkins."

David stood. "No, Your Honor, this is Miss Sadie Perkins, her daughter."

"Counselor, I thought we discussed this. I must examine Mrs. Eugenia Perkins if I am to determine the ownership of the property."

"I understand." David tugged his jacket and stood as straight as Sadie had ever seen anyone. "And, if you will permit me some leeway, I will be happy to show you why Mrs. Perkins is not present today."

The judge grumbled. "You will find that my patience is not long enduring. You best get to it quickly."

"Your Honor," Mr. Collins said as he jerked to his feet. "That is not what we decided. I object."

Judge Smithers leveled a hard gaze on Mr. Collins. "I suggest you defer to your lawyer. Unless, that is, you intend to represent yourself?"

The man beside Mr. Collins whispered something and the banker sat, still rather agitated. It was no matter. Her and David's chances were still slim at best. Mr. Collins need not worry so. But to look at David, he didn't believe that. He fairly exuded confidence.

"If you will allow it, Judge," David said, shifting his weight. "I would like Dr. Norwood to give his testimony at this time."

Now the well-dressed man beside Mr. Collins stood. "Judge Smithers, we haven't even given opening arguments. This is highly irregular."

The judge held up a hand. "So is Mr. Anderson by defying my direct order for him to produce Mrs. Perkins."

Sadie watched as the rather elongated man on the dais rubbed his chin.

He then set his hand back on the table provided to him. "But I am curious. I will allow it."

David held out an arm toward Dr. Norwood. The physician then shifted to stand.

"Dr. Norwood, I presume?" Judge Smithers entreated.

"Yes, Judge?" Dr. Norwood adjusted his jacket.

"Please, come." The judge indicated a chair near the dais. "You are the town doctor?"

Dr. Norwood settled into the chair, "Yes, Your Honor."

"For how many years?"

"Probably ten. Or there abouts."

Judge Smithers gave a brief nod. "What is the nature of your testimony?"

The doctor looked at David and then at Sadie.

Her chest tightened, and she let out a breath. Had she been holding it? Though the release of air did not ease the pressure in her chest. This was their best chance, according to David. And everything had to go just right.

"I am Mrs. Eugenia Perkins' doctor. And have been for some years. She is not mentally capable of appearing before a lawman."

The room was filled with gasps and a rumble of conversing.

Dr. Norwood looked at her again, and she tried to keep her posture stiff and her features set. She did not want to risk the doctor feeling as if he betrayed them. For he only spoke true.

Judge Smithers slammed his gavel again. "Quiet!"

The room quickly fell silent.

"You are telling me that the woman is mad?" The judge glared at the doctor.

"Yes. Her mind has been deteriorating over the last three years. And it has become worse in these last two or three months."

The judge looked from David to Sadie and back. "And there's no possible way she can answer questions?"

"Judge, anything she said—were it to even make sense—could not be trusted. She has lost her ability to discern memories—between past and present. And, on occasion, has even endangered herself and others."

The judge's brows arched then lowered, as if he worked to determine his next course of action. "I suppose we have no choice then but to hear Miss Sadie Perkins' testimony on these matters."

Mr. Collins shot out of his seat. "Your Honor!"

Judge Smithers held up a hand. "I have made my decision. I will hear her."

"Judge, I don't think you understand. This is a trick...a...a distraction from the facts."

The judge set his gaze on the man. "I advised you before to let your lawyer speak for you. And now I'm advising you to sit down."

Mr. Collins shifted and opened his mouth as if he would argue. The man to his right tugged at his sleeve.

"Now." The judge's eyes narrowed. "Or I'll have you thrown in jail for contempt."

The man all but fell into his seat, glowering.

"Miss Perkins." The judge lightened his tone, but only slightly. "You may take Dr. Norwood's seat."

Dr. Norwood stood and waited for Sadie.

She wasn't sure how this would come out. But the judge had been reasonable with what they had put forth. Maybe he would be reasonable with her. Though she prayed she wouldn't have to answer prying questions about her mother. It was difficult enough to hear the doctor expose Mother's situation to the town's ridicule. Could she?

David touched her arm but briefly. She didn't want to chance looking at him. Could she hold herself together if she did?

Rising, she maneuvered around the table and to the proffered chair.

Dr. Norwood helped her settle and then stepped back to his seat.

"Miss Perkins," the judge said, watching her, "Tell me about your mother's addled mind."

David sucked in a breath. The judge continuing to probe about Mrs. Perkins' condition had always been a possibility in his mind. But one he had hoped wouldn't come to fruition. He hated this for Sadie, yet he knew something she didn't. She was stronger than she gave herself credit for. And he believed in her.

That, however, didn't keep him from tensing. How could anyone watch the woman he loved in anguish and not?

"My mother's condition?" Sadie's voice broke as she spoke.

"Yes, Miss Perkins." The judge offered nothing further, no clarification, no real question. Just left it open for Sadie to speak.

Sadie looked to David.

He kept himself in check but tried to encourage her with his eyes.

"Look at me, Miss Perkins." There was a hard edge to Judge Smithers' voice.

Sadie cleared her throat. "My mother is a good woman." She hesitated, and David worried that she might not be able to be frank. But she continued. "But she has become rather...confused. About many things."

"Confused?" The judge arched a brow.

David swallowed. That wasn't enough. Sadie had to push through her fear. He did not relish bringing this about—she was afraid of the townsfolk, their opinions, their actions...and what may happen to her mother. That made sense. But he needed her to be honest. That was their only hope.

"She..." Sadie paused again.

She wasn't going to do it. David gripped his pen tightly. Until his hand ached.

Please, Sadie. You can do hard things. I know you can.

Sadie closed her eyes, drew in a breath, and spoke. "My mother can no longer remember the simplest things. Whether or not I am still in school, where things in the house are, the fact that my father..." Her voice caught. "...left us."

The judge continued to watch in silence. Would he not end the torture with something...anything?

"She injured her leg on the stairs, as she is troubled with balance. And only two days ago, she..." Sadie stopped herself.

Go on. David pled with her. Hoping that even silently, she could hear his heart.

"She set our home on fire."

There was a collective intake of breath. But the crowd minded the judge's earlier directive for quiet.

Judge Smithers' eyes widened. "Set the house on fire?"

"Yes, Your Honor."

There was no denying the emotion welling in Sadie. Indeed, she wiped at her cheek. Had she started tearing up?

"I do apologize for making you answer these questions, Miss Perkins. But it is imperative we get to the truth." The judge leaned back in his seat.

Sadie nodded. Though David doubted she truly understood the man's motives.

"Can you continue?" Judge Smithers set his hands on the table.

"Yes, Judge. I believe so."

His brave Sadie. This would not break her.

"What is your knowledge, if any, of the property on which you and your mother reside?"

"Your Honor, I object!" This time it was the lawyer for Mr. Collins. But one look at the banker's reddened face was enough to discern who the objection really came from.

The judge didn't so much as glance in that direction, just waved the lawyer down with a hand. "Miss Perkins?"

Sadie played with her hands in her lap. "The house and land were a part of my mother's inheritance, received before she married my father."

"And...if that is so, how do you have knowledge of it?"

"My father, at times, was rather verbose about his frustration that Mother had ownership of the property. It didn't mean much to me at the time. Not until...until he had embezzled any and all funds he could get his hands on."

Judge Smithers nodded.

"Your Honor, I insist that we have the opportunity to question Miss Perkins," the other lawyer said rather forcefully.

Only then did the judge look at the opposing side of the room. "That will not be necessary. I have made my determination."

That was likely a good thing for them, David realized. But he wanted desperately to comfort and support Sadie in some way. But he couldn't from this distance.

"Miss Perkins," Judge Smithers looked at her. "Mr. Anderson," he added, glancing at David.

David stood and indicated to Sadie with a hand that she should as well. She rose, rather unsteadily.

"Two things," the judge said. "I am satisfied that the house and surrounding property are your mother's solely. And it is apparent that

Mrs. Eugenia Perkins' mind is addled to the point she can no longer exercise her authority over herself or her property. Therefore, Miss Sadie Perkins will be granted guardianship over the estate."

Sadie let out a breath. As did David.

"Furthermore, it is my determination that Mrs. Perkins shall be taken from her home to an institution where she can receive the proper care and prevent any further endangerment of herself and others."

Sadie gripped the back of the chair. Would she collapse?

David could no longer maintain his distance, he rushed to her side and assisted her as she settled into the chair once more. This, too, was something he had feared.

"Your Honor, I beg a reprieve. Surely, the woman is well cared for in her home."

"I daresay she is not. She nearly burned the place down—with herself and her loved ones inside." The judge's stern gaze was unyielding. "Either she is surrendered to a proper institution within twenty-four hours, or Sheriff McAllen will place her under arrest. For her safety as much as anyone's."

The voices of the crowd behind swelled.

"That is all," Judge Smithers said, banging his gavel one last time before rising and moving toward the building's exit.

The volume of the townsfolk grew as they moved to press in.

He had to get Sadie out of here.

She had hunched over on the chair, wracked with emotion.

He gripped her hand as he crouched. "We have to go."

She did not fight him as he gathered her to his side and fought their way through the suffocating mass and out of the church.

CHAPTER 23

The Chance

W hat was Sadie going to do? She couldn't surrender her mother. She just couldn't. Not to one of those god-forsaken, horrid places.

She was perched on her settee, watching David pace in the parlor.

All this time, she had fought and struggled to keep Mother home and safe. Now, she had saved one only to lose the other. And it was not the one she would have chosen. She had trusted David. How could this have happened?

Though as she looked at him, clearly in distress, she couldn't really fault him. He had done what he could. And he hadn't left yet. Would he stay by her side until they worked this out and saved Mother from the terrible fate ascribed to her? It wasn't even a question. He loved her. She knew he would not abandon her.

"There must be some way..." he said as he continued to wear a path in the floor.

"I don't know." Yet even as she spoke the words, she wished she could unsay them. She sounded defeated. Was she?

Aunt Jane stepped through the open door with a tray. "I thought some tea would be in order." She offered Sadie a sweet smile, but the levity didn't make it to her eyes. There, Sadie read the sadness reflected from her own eyes.

"Thank you," Sadie said. If nothing else, there were her manners.

Aunt Jane stepped toward her, squeezed her hand briefly, and turned to leave.

Leave. Yes, Aunt Jane would be leaving tomorrow. Sadie was glad for it, even as the thought of her dear aunt's absence brought a deepening to the ever-present ache in her chest. But there was no reason for Aunt Jane to stay. Mother would already be committed to the asylum by the time the stage left tomorrow. What more was there for Aunt Jane here? She had been right before; it was time she returned home. For certain, there were things to tend to. Besides, that meant Alice would be leaving, and that had been sorely needed. Sadie's cousin had been nothing but heartache and trouble.

David stopped his pacing and looked at Sadie. "I need to send a telegram to my practice. Perhaps one of others knows of some recourse."

The thought of his not being here gave her pause. Yes, he needed to go. But how would she hold it together without his strength to comfort her?

He stepped to her and, crouching, took her hands. "I will be back as quickly as I can."

She nodded but had to bite at her lip to keep it from quivering. Had all her strength left her? Indeed, this day had been difficult, but she was stronger than this. She had to be. For in a matter of days, he might leave for good. He had a life back in Richmond.

Dismay threatened to wash over her. But she needed to trust him. And trust in God's goodness. If nothing else, God would make a way.

David leaned forward and brushed a kiss across her cheek.

She craved more, but he pulled back and extricated his hold on her.

He paused at the doorway to the parlor, as if unsure he would go. Then he looked back. "We will figure this out. I promise it."

She nodded but couldn't stop the tears as he turned and moved away.

Walking away from Sadie had pained David. She was so vulnerable right now. So much in need of his support. But he needed her, too. To assure himself that she didn't hate him after he had failed her.

If he were honest with himself, this was always how it would have gone. At best.

The judge could not have, in wisdom, made any other decision. But there had to be another option for them. There had to be.

David dismounted near the telegraph office and strode in. He greeted the operator and penned a brief question to his law firm before handing it over.

The telegraph operator raised a brow at the message but made no comment as he turned toward his instruments. "I'll get this sent right away."

"Thank you." David turned to exit.

The man called after him, halting him. "Oh, there's a telegram for you, as well."

David supposed he should have expected as much. But he wasn't ready to receive his father's ire. He grabbed for the paper and read it. An ultimatum—come home or lose any prospect, any interest in the law firm.

What was he going to do? He couldn't return as Sadie was surrendering her mother. He couldn't leave when she needed support the most.

And he paused. He had already given up and decided that there was nothing that could be done. How could he encourage Sadie in such a state?

But, deep down, he knew there was no legal standing they might take to allow for them to overturn the judge's decision. Certainly not in twenty-four hours.

He wasn't much given to prayer. And his faith could be rather small. Practical, more tangible things made more sense to him. But was there harm in seeking the Lord? *Father, if there is a way, can You show me?*

There was too much to consider in this telegram from his father. Too much weighing on each choice. And if there was any hope of keeping Mrs. Perkins out of the asylum, he needed to be here, helping

Sadie. How could it be that she became more important than his partnership at the firm? Indeed, he did love her. Very much.

He moved toward his horse. What would he say to her? What could he say but the truth?

"Mr. Anderson!" a voice beseeched him from farther down the planked sidewalk.

He turned to see Dr. Norwood coming toward him at the quickest polite pace anyone could manage.

David gripped his horse's reins and waited for the doctor's awkward steps to bring him closer. "Dr. Norwood, I want to thank you for your—"

"There's no time for that." The doctor shook his head. "I have something urgent. I may have an amenable solution, but there is need for haste."

Hope blossomed in David's being. "Tell me."

CHAPTER 24

Happiness

David knocked on the front door, about to go out of his skin in desperation to see Sadie. The events that had begun unfolding had him too elated for much patience. And in that swell, he again came to see how deeply he cared for Sadie. There was no chance he could continue without her. Even as things with her mother may be soon settled, he had no desire to leave her.

In that lay another decision he had made.

Mrs. Wallem opened the door.

He nodded to the woman in greeting. "Where is Sadie?" His words were more breathless than he'd have liked. But after the quick ride back to the Perkins' estate, it couldn't be helped.

"She's still in the parlor."

He didn't wait for her to usher him within. Stepping around Mrs. Wallem, he rushed farther into the house.

As he came to the parlor door, he did find Sadie as he had left her. Though, her body shook slightly as she looked at the scenery beyond the window.

"Sadie," he breathed.

She turned. Her eyes were reddened, and her whole being quivered. It broke him.

He crossed the room and all but fell to the floor, kneeling in front of her. "Sadie, I have news."

She wiped at her tears.

"Dr. Norwood is on his way here now. He has contact with a doctor who has some kind of home for those like your mother. Those in need of special care."

"But..." she started, her features scrunching.

"It is not like the institutions. The doctor provides a safe home for those in such a condition. He treats them, cares for them. Dr. Norwood trusts the man."

Sadie's mouth moved, but she seemed unsure of what to say.

"That's not all," he softened his tone and reached for her hands.

Her eyebrows lifted.

"I know this is fast. And I know this may not be the best way to do this. I would rather have candlelight and music...you deserve all of that."

Her brows furrowed.

"But with this news forthcoming, I want you to know that I will be by your side. Every step of the way. No matter where it takes us. No matter what happens with the law firm. I will be with you."

Her brow smoothed, and her eyes glistened. "What are you saying?"

"I want to marry you, Sadie. I want to wake up every day to a life we build together."

She swallowed.

His heart seemed to stop beating for a moment.

"So much is uncertain. I don't know what will happen with Mother. I don't know what Dr. Norwood will say. Or where I will go." Then she smiled. "But I want to be with you. No matter what. So, yes, David. I will marry you."

His whole body warmed, and he gathered her to himself as she stood, crushing his mouth to hers. He held her as if to never let go. In fact, he hoped that would be the case. And he let himself get lost in the moment.

Sadie held onto David's shoulders as she sunk into him. Could they stay like this forever?

A throat clearing near the door brought her back to reality. And she pulled back.

Dr. Norwood stood at the entrance to the parlor, fighting a grin.

Her face heated, but she did not truly regret kissing David. Not even knowing that they had been caught.

David released her and stepped toward the doctor. "I told her everything you told me. But you promised the details would be forthcoming."

Dr. Norwood nodded.

"Doctor, is it true? A hope for my mother to be cared for well?"

"Yes." The doctor moved farther into the parlor toward Sadie. "And I received final word from him just now. There is a place for her in the home."

Sadie's spirit lifted. But there was still much she didn't know. Where would it take them? She needed to be near Mother. How would she and David make a life elsewhere? But, with him by her side, she would go anywhere.

"Well, where is it? When will she be able to go?" David's questions seemed to tumble out.

The doctor's smile widened. "She can go as soon as she is prepared. It's in Hopewell, Virginia."

"Hopewell?" David had a wonder about his voice as he spoke the word.

"Where is that?" Sadie wished she could be part of whatever transpired between the men.

"It's just outside of Richmond." David looked at her, and his eyes fairly shone. He would be able to maintain his work with his firm or go off on his own. His options were now open.

"I need to speak with Mrs. Wallem," Sadie said, reluctant to walk away from David in this moment. But she had to inform the older woman about the changes of the last hour.

"Let me do that." Dr. Norwood blocked the doorway. "I think you two have some things to discuss." The doctor smiled at the two before turning and moving off.

"Can God really be so good?" David's words seemed full of wonder and disbelief.

Sadie faced him and settled her hands on his chest. "I believe He is."

David claimed her lips once more. This time, as the rush of sensation moved through her, she knew she had found her place. With him.

Epilogue

David smiled at his cousin beside him. Brandon and Amanda had been more than gracious these last few days... not to mention Aunt Sylvia's patience with delaying their return to Richmond for a bit longer. And what a harried few days it had been! But David refused to wait any longer for Sadie to be his bride.

They had sent Mrs. Wallem and Mrs. Perkins on to Hopewell with notes from Dr. Norwood, and then the plans for the wedding came together without distraction. One would think the Millers had adopted Sadie the way they came around her and fussed over her.

She deserved every bit of it. For her journey these last months had been difficult.

Their fight for the property, it seemed, would go to a greater cause. Cutie and Mariena had needed a place to set up their school for the Indian children. And Sadie graciously offered the estate. Even in the midst of everything, Sadie had blessed others with her generous nature. Some of the townsfolk had come around to see that Sadie was not responsible for her father's actions, but many held to their anger...and their judgments. He was glad he would be taking her away from this place.

His reverie was interrupted as the piano's tempo changed. And now Sadie appeared, in a cream and gold dress, walking toward him.

Brandon set a hand to his shoulder with a gentle squeeze. Did he seem to have needed that? Though he did appreciate the way it grounded him. With Sadie coming down the makeshift aisle in the field beyond the church, he might very well float away.

She smiled as she neared and slid her hands into his.

They were ready to face the future, whatever it held, together.

Keep reading for a preview of the first book in the Cripple Creek Series!

Thank you, dear reader, for for reading along with me! If you enjoyed this story, I would sincerely appreciate if you would submit a review. It would mean so much to me!

To read more about these characters, follow along with the Convenient Risk Series. Find it at:
https://saraturnquist.com/convenient-risk-series/

Author's Note

I do hope you have enjoyed this addition to the CONVENIENT RISK SERIES. These characters have a piece of my heart for certain.

Continuing in the only somewhat fictional town of Wharton City in southeastern Arizona, we have opened up to some newer characters: David and Sadie. David was introduced in *These Golden Years* and Sadie is the daughter of the banker from *A Convenient Risk*, though she was never "seen" on the pages of that novel.

This novel touches on the state of mental illness awareness and care during the late 1800's. Asylums and sanitarium-type facilities, or "madhouses," were built on the outskirts of major cities and they were the only option really to care for these individuals. The conditions in these places were, I'm sure, as good as could be managed with what funding and understanding existed, but they were not truly the ideal situations for those suffering. Though they were better than jail, which is where some individuals defined as "lunatics" ended up. Medication for the treatment of mental ailments was also in its infancy. Often, mental illness was viewed as demonic possession and would be treated with exorcism. Shock therapy and/or lobotomies were also commonplace for these individuals.

There were also advancements, as you may have noted in the book, in legal rights for married women. This allowed for some leeway in the story. Laws were being written and passed in New York and Massachusetts most notably among other places, that gave married women some rights over the property they brought into the marriage. This would have been a fairly new development at the time.

As I enjoy history, the realities I find can sometimes be hard to understand and difficult to swallow. But I choose to let it lend itself to thankfulness for what advancements and progress have been made in these areas.

The stagecoach moved along, bumping and rocking as it went. Trees and other green scenery whisked by the window. Views of mountains and open plains were visible from the seat of the coach, vistas familiar to its occupant. Katherine Matthews was coming home.

She returned to Cripple Creek, no longer the scared, unsure teenager who had left to further her education so many years ago with hopes and dreams of a new life in a new place. No, she had matured into a confident young woman who had grown in stature and in beauty. Her hair was no longer the mousy color she always hated, for it had deepened into the same beautiful chestnut brown she had always admired in her mother's appearance. She'd grown out of her awkward teenage features, and was now well regarded among her peers as a rather handsome woman.

Returning to Cripple Creek brought many rather-mixed emotions to the surface. Imagine, one of her first postings would be at the same schoolhouse where she received her educational start. When her mother wrote to her of the interim need, she was glad to help out. What an odd coincidence that the letter would find her, too, in transition. Would this turn into a permanent placement? Did she want it to?

The mountain scenery became more recognizable, and she thought back on her childhood. There were so many happy times here. Unbidden, her mind wandered to the day of the great tragedy that had marred her spirit—the day Ellie Mae died.

Even all these years later, she carried the scar in her heart. The events of that day had left her broken. Why must thoughts of Ellie Mae plague her so? And all the more as her return became imminent? She shivered as the images from her nightmares the previous evening flitted across her mind. They would not stop. These same visions visited her in sleep night after night. All the more frequently these last weeks.

Closing her eyes, the hazy images took form and became memory. It was as if no time had passed. She and Ellie, walking through the schoolyard just as they did every other day . . .

Hooking arms with Ellie Mae, Katherine stepped out of the schoolhouse and into the yard. A rather large group of students gathered off to the right near the old tree. It didn't bother Katherine. She turned her attention toward the path that would lead home.

"What do you think they're up to?" Ellie Mae whispered.

Katherine glanced in that direction and noticed Betsy Callaway at the center, flapping her jaws. Why would anyone listen to anything she said? But they did. The class at large seemed to adore Betsy. It didn't make sense. Clenching her teeth, Katherine grabbed for Ellie Mae's hand. "Whatever it is, we don't want to be involved." She pulled Ellie Mae along as she walked on, trying to pass the gathering.

"I know Miss Matthews couldn't do it," Betsy said loudly.

Katherine froze in her tracks. What had she just said?

The crowd of students parted and glared at Katherine and Ellie Mae.

"Let's keep going," Ellie Mae pleaded, tugging on Katherine's hand.

She should listen to Ellie Mae and not become a part of whatever game Betsy played. But she could not let Betsy get the best of her. What would everyone think of her?

So, she turned to face her accuser. There stood Betsy with Wyatt Sullivan, the most popular boy in school, right beside her. Betsy's blonde pigtails, tied back with perfect pink ribbons, shone in the sun. Her dress was no less perfect, pink with just the right amount of lace and even a slight puff to the sleeves.

"Do what, pray tell?" Katherine shot back. Her heart beat furiously in her chest.

"Go down through the mine shaft." Betsy folded her arms in front of her chest and raised an eyebrow.

Katherine's heart skipped a beat then, but she tried not to show her fear.

Ellie Mae's grip tightened on her hand.

"I assure you, Miss Callaway, it's not that I can't do it. It's simply that I have better things to do than to be traipsing about a mine shaft." She turned to leave and hoped that would be enough to silence Betsy.

"Prove it." Betsy's voice rang out after her.

Katherine's eyes slid closed. Was there any way around this? "I have nothing to prove to you," she called back over her shoulder.

"Fraidycat!" Betsy laughed.

The other students joined in.

Katherine's face burned. A fire had been lit within her. She was not afraid of anything! Releasing Ellie Mae's hand, she then whirled around. "I am not afraid!"

"There's only one way we'll believe that." Betsy's hands moved from her chest to her hips.

There was no way this would be a one-way challenge. "Are you going?" Katherine poked her chin out, putting her own hands on her hips, attempting to puff up her chest as much as she could.

"Of course," Betsy said, though her voice caught.

"Then, let's go." Katherine grabbed after Ellie Mae's hand and headed out in the direction of the old mine shaft. She hoped Ellie Mae didn't feel how her palms had started to sweat. Perspiration covered her whole body. How was she to keep up this façade?

The group of students followed, a din of voices behind. As they neared the cavernous opening, they became quiet as they halted several feet short of the forbidden place.

Wyatt pushed through the crowd once they had stopped. "Now, girls, this is foolishness. Talking about it is one thing, but you're not actually going down there, are you?"

Katherine glanced at the mine opening. It looked dark and ominous. Not what she wanted to see. Then she eyed Betsy. She had everything—the popularity, the most handsome boy in school ... But she would not have Katherine's pride, too. "I am."

"Then I am, too." Betsy stared at Katherine, matching her glare through slitted eyes.

"Kath-rine," Ellie whispered, tugging on her hand.

Katherine looked over at her friend. Ellie's eyes begged her not to go. Katherine wondered again at the danger. Her friend had every right to be concerned, she supposed. But it would not last. Betsy would go but a few steps in and give up. Katherine was sure of it. So, she would not be dissuaded.

Wyatt's eyes moved from one girl to the other. A couple of years older than the girls at their thirteen years, he stood a good head taller than Katherine. At last, he threw his hands up in the air. "Then I'm going too."

"And so am I," came Ellie Mae's quiet response.

Katherine leaned toward her friend. "Ellie, you don't have to go." Her eyes held Ellie's. What was she going to do? She couldn't take Ellie into that place. But something had eased in her when Ellie Mae volunteered to go. Was it selfish of her to want her friend to accompany her?

"Yes, I do." Her voice was firm, though her chin quivered. "I'm sticking with you."

A bump in the trail jolted Katherine from her reverie. The scenery outside became blurred. Or was it her? Touching her face, she felt moisture. She wiped at the tears. This would not do! Whatever happened when she returned, Katherine was determined she would face it with as much bravery as she could muster.

To read more, find *Hope in Cripple Creek* here:

https://saraturnquist.com/hope-in-cripple-creek/

A Convenient Risk (Book 1)

He never imagined her heart would be so hard to reach.

Forced into a marriage of convenience after her husband dies, Amanda is determined she will never love again. Brandon only needs her husband's cattle. Butting heads over the decisions of the ranch, add to their frustration. Their new family's well being is soon threatened as their lives become entangled with Billy the Kid and his gang.

What has she gotten herself into? What kind of man has she married? Is there any way out?

An Inconvenient Christmas (Book 2)

Brandon and Amanda are ready for their "Happily Ever After". This Christmas will be a time to share with their little family and maybe experience some much needed peace on earth. That's when the letter comes. And everything is turned upside-down. Nothing is as it should be and tensions mount.

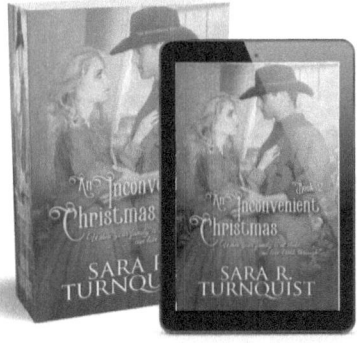

Will they make it through this holiday season unscathed? Or will they be torn apart by the time Christmas Day comes?

A Less Convenient Path (Book 3)

She is in a hopeless situation. He doesn't have a chance.

Mariena's native nation has been ordered to a Reservation but her tribe was attacked en route. She and her young brother wander in a wilderness filled with dangerous animals. Until...

Cutie happens upon them as he flees his own demons. Can Mariena awaken something he never expected? Even bring him to believe in himself once more?

A story of two people without peace. Will they find in each other the very things they are missing?

A Convenient Escape (Book 4)

She has nowhere to go. He has nothing to lose.

Lily has known hardship and rejection. Her brother takes a job at the Miller ranch. Now with no ally, she becomes desperate to get away...by any means necessary.

Dan is prepared to do whatever it takes to ensure Lily is cared for... even if that means proposing marriage.

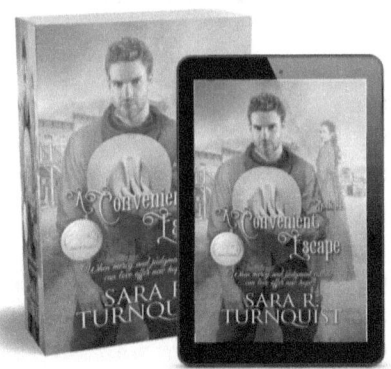

Will they make it to the church? Or find themselves victims of lies, disillusionment, or the ire of an Apache rebel?

An Inconvenient Acquaintance (Book 5)

She wants adventure. He needs a place to belong.

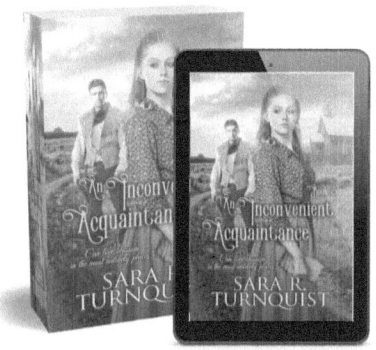

Ada the new schoolteacher in Tombstone. Her desire for independence stems from tales of the west. But she never expected to find herself torn between two men—one who promises safety and security, the other's future is uncertain and offers excitement.

Slim is determined that he will not become involved with a woman of privilege, Ada's fiery personality intrigues him. And soon he is vying for her heart with a man he'd rather not trifle with.

Will they find what they seek in each other? Or will they become caught up in a shootout at the O.K. Corral?

These Golden Years (Book 6)

A collection of short stories through the year.

Dorothy "Cook" Miller and "Uncle" Owen Miller are living their best life and marriage. Though it is not without bumps along the way. Join them as they walk through the year together with its measure of mishaps and laughs. This collection of short stories shows that marriage can be fraught with misunderstanding. But also has its share of lighter moments.

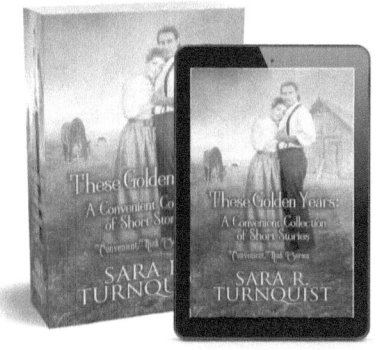

An Less Convenient Arrangement (Book 7)

She has lost all hope. He has little desire to stay by her side.

Sadie finds herself in dire straits after her father absconds with everyone's money. Her mother's failing mental stability also becomes a trial she is not certain she can overcome. Is there anywhere she can turn?

Though his one goal is to return to Richmond and a partnership in his father's law firm, David is drawn to Sadie and softens to her plight. He offers what help he can, but resists being pulled into the mess that has become her life. Until he starts to care beyond that initial attraction.

Can she stand strong against the challenges facing her?
Will David risk following his heart regardless of the cost?
Or take the first out offered to him?

Ranch Hands Collection

Four Stories from the Miller Ranch

Acknowledgments

It's that time again...time to remember how so many have touched this book and led to its creation and existance. And there have been many. Perhaps more than I can name!

My editor, Julie Sherwood, you continue to push me to be a better writer and story crafter. And you catch my typos. Thank goodness!

Cora Graphics, my cover artist, is just phenomenal. There is no other word to describe her. I am impressed by both her talent and how easy she is to work with.

My narrator, Becky Brabham, you bring so much to my books! You bring these characters to life in amazing ways. You never cease to amaze me with your range and abilities.

My craft partner, Kelly Hollman, who has read every word and contributed to this work in innumerable ways. You encourage me and hold me accountable. And I appreciate that more than you know!

I also can't get by without mentioning my Word Weavers critique group. You have read my scenes and given feedback that has sharpened my work.

My photographer, Rachel Bull, who makes this crazy hair look stylish, is also one of the most talented people I know.

For my sister, you make me want to be better. For my dad, you make me feel so good to have achieved this dream of writing. For my mom, I will love you forever. And for my husband and kids, you give me every reason to smile.

Last, but certainly not least, my readers, you give me a reason to keep writing.

About the Author

Sara is a coffee lovin', word slinging, Historical Romance author whose super power is converting caffeine into novels. She loves those odd little tidbits of history that are stranger than fiction. That's what inspires her. Well, that and a good love story.

But of all the love stories she knows, hers is her favorite. She lives happily with her own Prince Charming and their gaggle of minions. Three to be exact. They sure know how to distract a writer! But, alas, the stories must be written, even if it must happen in the wee hours of the morning.

Sara is an avid reader and enjoys reading and writing clean Historical Romance when she's not traveling.

Please follow along with her journey through her newsletter at: http://saraturnquist.com/list

Happy Reading!

SARA R. TURNQUIST

Author
Editor
Speaker

 facebook.com/AuthorSaraRTurnquist

 instagram.com/sararturnquist

 x.com/sararturnquist

 youtube.com/@SaraRTurnquist

 pinterest.com/sararturnquist

Also by Sara R. Turnquist

www.ingramcontent.com/pod-product-compliance
Lightning Source LLC
Chambersburg PA
CBHW031443200726
48289CB00007BB/2186